Spice Islands Mystery

Not for... S0-BBJ-296

ALICE POYNOR

0 0 0 0 2 7 2 2

AN OMF BOOK

© Overseas Missionary Fellowship
(formerly China Inland Mission)
Published by
Overseas Missionary Fellowship (IHQ) Ltd.
2 Cluny Road, Singapore 1025, Republic of Singapore.

First published 1989

OMF BOOKS are distributed by
OMF, 404 South Church Street,
    Robesonia, PA 19551. USA
OMF, Belmont, The Vine,
    Sevenoaks, Kent, TN13 3TZ, UK
OMF, P O Box 849, Epping,
    NSW 2121. Australia
OMF, 1058 Avenue Road, Toronto,
    Ontario M5N 206, Canada
OMF, P O Box 10159, Balmoral,
    Auckland, New Zealand
OMF, P O Box 41,
    Kenilworth 7745. South Africa
and other OMF offices.

This story is set in Indonesia in the late 1970s.

ISBN 99781-972-82-4

CONTENTS

CHAPTER

ONE

T he voice of the stewardess came smoothly over the intercom,

"Ladies and gentlemen, we have arrived at Jakarta International Airport. We ask you to remain seated until the plane has reached the terminal and has come to a complete stop. It has been a pleasure serving you on Garuda Indonesia Airways and we hope you enjoy your visit to Indonesia."

I put away *Mystery at Ghost Rock Lighthouse,* collected my jacket and bag and followed Dad down the steps of the 747. The heat whacked me in the face as I stepped onto the tarmac, reminding me that I was standing almost directly on the equator.

Taxis honked, tour guides bubbled out announcements, and Chinese, westerners, Indians and of course homecoming Indonesians poured off the plane, creating a babble of languages and a fashion show of international garb.

The whole picture blurred and buzzed around me in a jumbled sensation of strangeness as I followed my parents into the terminal. I was only half aware of all that was going on. It had been yesterday when we boarded the plane in Milwaukee, Wisconsin, and I'd had little sleep since. There were the drinks, followed by meals, followed by air turbulence, followed by movies, and on and on. My stomach was a little queasy and I wanted to crawl into the nearest bed and sleep for a week.

I shifted my bag to the other shoulder and pulled out my passport. Inside the blue and silver cover proclaiming "United States of America" was my not-too-flattering picture showing my freckles and making my face look fat. It made me look younger than my twelve years, too, which I heartily resented. Nevertheless, the vital statistics were there. Name: Alan Gregory Carter. Sex: M. Place of birth: Wisconsin, USA. Date of birth: December 11. Hair: brown. Eyes: grey.

"Hey," Debbie squawked, "quit shoving me. I can't move anywhere."

"Sorry," I muttered. I was too tired to put up with my sister bugging me. "Move your guitar then; it's poking into me." I don't know why she insisted on bringing so much junk anyway.

The line to go through immigration wasn't moving very quickly. At least it was cool inside the terminal.

"I hope Uncle Phil and Aunt Lori's house will be this cool," I said to Mom. "If we're going to stay for two weeks I want a temperature that supports human existence. Not like it was outside."

"Well, it won't be *this* cool. They don't have airconditioning. But with fans you'll be surprised how comfortable it'll be."

"You should know better than that," Debbie said. "They're missionaries, remember? They won't have anything." I was afraid she was right.

Just then an announcement interrupted the general airport clamor and I perked up my ears. After saying something in Indonesian, a lady's voice said, "Announcing the arrival of Singapore Airlines flight 602 from Singapore at gate L-3."

Just as she said that, a Singapore Airlines airbus pulled into the terminal at the large window to my right. Two policemen walked past and stopped in front of the desk at the L-3 area.

"Hey, Deb, look. I wonder what those police are doing."

The door opened and passengers filed out in twos and threes, most laden with shopping bags and bulging handbags. As I watched the police stepped forward.

I poked Debbie and whispered, "Look, they're after that guy."

The police had a man between them and were walking him over to the desk beside the one where we were waiting. His face was half-hidden under a heavy lock of hair that dipped over his forehead half an inch above his mirror sunglasses. Other than that the only thing I remember about his face was a mole on his left cheek. He was well-dressed and I especially noticed his briefcase. Some kind of skin – snakeskin maybe or alligator – anyway it was impressive. He was remarkably calm I thought, under the circumstances, almost like he was used to this.

"Wonder what they're looking for," Debbie said to me. They had the man put his briefcase up on the ticket desk and the police were going through his papers. As they opened the lid I got a good look at the initials, TRA, in gold on the top. In a few minutes the police seemed satisfied, closed the briefcase and left.

"I wonder what that was all about."

"Maybe he's a smuggler."

"Maybe. Or he didn't have the right passport or visa or something."

"Well, whatever it is, maybe I should help them." I cleared my throat and added in the most official tone I could muster, "With my skill in all matters legal, I might be of assistance in apprehending a large-scale perpetrator." I felt some of my lethargy slipping away at the thought of possibly putting my detective skills to work.

"Oh, sure," Deb said, sarcastically. "Always trying to make a mystery out of nothing. That's what you get when all you read is mystery and detective stuff."

"It's not all I read."

"Almost. Anyway whatever it is has nothing to do with us."

Mmm. Maybe. Maybe not. I admit I do have a tendency to be a bit dramatic. Mom's always telling me that. And I do enjoy a good detective story.

Actually I think it's made me more observant. I like trying to remember details as if I were going to need them to solve a crime – even though I never do.

"I can see what you mean about losing weight in this climate," Dad said to Mom. "I could feel the pounds melting off when we were out on the tarmac."

"Great!" Debbie said. "I hope I lose five." She's already skinny but it seems to be her constant concern. "Maybe even Alan will go home with a little less blubber," she said, grinning at me.

I'm not exactly the skinny type. Never have been. Since I started Junior High and started playing baseball I've lost a little fat but I'm still pretty solid. "That's muscle, all muscle," I told Debbie.

"I bet you're fatter than Steve," she said. Of course I would be fatter than Steve; he's always been the shape of a piece of string. Steve McDonald is my cousin who's a little older than I am.

I ignored her remark as it was our turn through immigration by this time so we showed our passports and answered the necessary questions and left the terminal. We had nearly five hours till the next plane left for Central Java, where the McDonalds live.

I need to explain. My mother lived in Indonesia until she was fifteen. Her dad, my grandfather, was an executive with a Dutch company. My grandparents are Dutch – well, I guess that makes Mom Dutch too, but I just think of her as American like the rest of us. Anyway she still remembered some

Indonesian language and knew the country well enough to show us around. It's a good thing; all I knew in Indonesian was three words. Anyway, one reason we decided to take this trip was so Mom would have a chance to show us where she grew up. And of course to visit my uncle and aunt.

I was a bit reluctant to go at first. I'd been playing baseball in the community league for one thing, and I had a chance of being in the all-stars this year. I didn't want to miss out on that. Also the last time Uncle Phil and Aunt Lori were home was three years ago, and then they lived in another part of the country so we only saw them twice the whole time. I knew them, but not well enough to get excited about visiting them.

Besides I really wasn't wild about seeing missionary work. At a missions conference, that's fine. I like seeing the stuff they show and the stories they tell. But who wants to spend their vacation on the mission field? Know what I mean? I figured there'd be no TV, nothing to do and nobody to do it with (sisters don't count), and miserable living conditions that would make army boot camp look like a resort.

Of course, all I knew about Indonesia you could write in half a page: used to be called the Spice Islands, sought after by Columbus for cinnamon and cloves and pepper, later ruled by Holland, called the Dutch East Indies, a long chain of islands on the equator. You know – the stuff you study in fifth grade. And a few personal tidbits my mother would tell from time to time.

But here I was and I might as well make the best of it. It was beginning to look like there might be some possibility for excitement even here.

CHAPTER

TWO

"We have a long time to wait. Why don't we get a taxi and see some of the sights before we leave Jakarta," Mom suggested. "I'd like to see Monas."

Monas is a tower with a gold flame on top of a tall pedestal, visible for a long way across the city. You can go inside the building and see the Pancasila, the Indonesian constitution. The really neat thing about it, as far as I'm concerned, is that this constitution is enclosed in a glass case that rolls into place and lights up for you to see when the guard pushes the button. Of course it's well guarded all the time. Anyway we had a look at it and the pictures on display, and went back out to cross the big park around the statue to get a taxi to the airport. As usual with a tourist attraction there were a lot of other people around, all moving in more or less the same direction.

Suddenly I heard a *whirr* behind me and turned just in time to see a boy about my age on a bike, coming straight through the crowd.

"Look out, Mom," I yelled. The bike skinned past me and around Mom who was walking just ahead of me, passing so close to her that it took her a minute to get her breath and realize what had happened.

"My bag! That boy's got my bag!"

Dad and I and a couple other men in the crowd took off running. The cyclist disappeared from view, but a few hundred yards ahead of us we saw him throw the bag on the grass as he rode away.

Dad reached it first. He picked the bag up and looked in it. "Everything's still here," he called to Mom. "Amazing. I can't see anything missing. Just rumpled a bit. I guess he decided with all of us on his tail it wasn't worth taking a chance, so he changed his mind and gave it up."

"Really? He didn't take my wallet?"

"No, it's here."

"Oh, wonderful! I guess you're right. He had second thoughts about it and got rid of it. Well, whatever the reason, I'm very glad."

Mom was still getting over the ordeal a while later when we got on the little Garuda Airways plane for Yogyakarta, a town in the middle of the island of Java. That's where Uncle Phil and Aunt Lori met us and drove us a couple hours' to where they live in Salatiga.

By the time we arrived at their house I felt like I'd gotten in the way of a steam roller. My clothes stuck to me, sweat trickled steadily down my forehead, my shoes rubbed holes in my heels and any

energy I'd ever had to begin with had long gone.
The air hung weighted and damp. Hardly a leaf
rustled, and the whole town seemed to be in sus-
pense waiting for something to melt through the
wall of heat. Mom said the summer time is the
rainy season, and that makes it hotter and stickier
than ever because things are so damp.

It was a treat to sit in the McDonalds' cool living
room, shoes off, overhead fan churning the air, cold
drink in hand and just collapse for a while. This
wasn't as bad as I'd thought. There was even a TV.
"Not that there's much on that's worth watching,"
Steve told me. "English programming for an hour
in the evenings, cartoons mostly, and sometimes a
show Sunday afternoon."

"I didn't even expect you to have anything that
modern," I said sheepishly.

"Oh, Indonesia's quite developed," Uncle Phil
said. "Especially the island of Java."

"I guess I'd kind of expected to see more poverty
everywhere," Dad said.

"Oh, no. The standard of living is quite high here
compared to some parts of the world," Uncle Phil
answered. "There's plenty of food, for one thing.
Bananas, papaya, pineapple, all grow easily everywhere. And vegetables in the higher areas. You
could hardly starve to death if you wanted to, under
normal conditions."

"Good!" I liked the sound of that. Food has
always rated high on my list of interests!

"And Indonesia puts a lot of emphasis on educa-
tion. The standard is constantly rising."

When I felt I could exert myself again, I un-packed my stuff in the room I was to share with Steve. In my suitcase, wrapped carefully in my underwear, I found the Swiss Army knife I'd bought just a week before I left home. It had cost me half a week's wages, seeing as I only work part time at the Burger Palace. But it was one thing I'd wanted ever since I saw it displayed at a Swiss product show in Wisconsin several years ago. I figured it was worth the money. I pulled it out, wiped its shiny red surface and put it in my pocket.

"Wow! That's quite a collection of planes you've got. Did you put them all together yourself?" I pointed to the models Steve had all around his room. They hung from the ceiling, sat on shelves, peeked from under a pile of papers on his desk. They were everywhere!

"Yeah. I like models. Any kind, but mostly air-craft. Look at this one. It's my newest. An F15 Eagle."

"Sleek. Those things are fast, aren't they? I saw one at an air show once and it took off straight up. Whoosh. Gone. Just like that."

"Yeah, they're awesome. They can actually go faster than mach 2."

I could see we were going to have a lot to do together. I asked about the plans for the next two weeks.

"Well, I won't be able to be with you all the time. I've got to leave for school in just a couple weeks," Steve answered. "And there's a lot of things I've got to do before then. But you'll find plenty to do and see and Bonar will be able to take you places."

"Who? Who's Bonar?" I didn't know if it was a dog or girlfriend or what.

"Bonar's the boy who works here. He came from Jakarta a few months ago looking for work and Dad hired him to help out around the place. He works part time for us, and goes to high school."

"So he lives here?"

"Yeah, out back there in the room near the kitchen. He's about my age. You'll like him."

"Does he speak English?"

"Yeah. They learn it in school and I've taught him more so now he's pretty good."

I wasn't exactly thrilled at the idea of having to be alone with this guy. I didn't know him, I couldn't speak his language and probably couldn't understand his English, I wouldn't know what to talk to him about...

I returned to my unpacking.

"How're things at school?" I asked Steve, changing the subject. "What kind of school d'you go to anyway?"

"A mission school. It's called Faith Academy, in the Philippines. All of the kids from our mission live together in a big house. We have neat houseparents and the school is great. I like it..."

"Don't you mind going away from home?"

"Not now. I did when I was younger. But all my friends are there. I like to come home, of course, but I'm always glad to go back when the time comes."

"Man! Must be some school."

"It's cooled off a bit now," Steve said to me. "Let's

go for a ride before supper. You can ride our extra bike."

We pulled out onto the main road. The train tracks ran alongside us and geese grazed nonchalantly beside them. Up ahead on the left I saw an old u-shaped wooden building with a tin roof and several smaller buildings back from the road.

"That's the former army camp," Steve explained. "It's deserted now. The new army camp is right behind it, facing on the other street, over there."

As we got closer he slowed his bike for me to come alongside of him. "Wonder why that *becak's** going down there. There's nothing down that road but the old camp, and like I say nobody uses it now."

As he pointed down the dirt road I could see a three wheeled bicycle pedaling toward the building. It had a seat behind it and a roof over the top. These overgrown tricycles were everywhere. I soon learned they were called *becaks.* I noticed this one had a blue plastic roof and two blue and white checked flags flying on antennae at the sides. A mock-licence plate wired on the back declared "I love Mama".

From the number we had already passed I knew plastic roofs and some kind of flags were common on these bicycle-taxis, but something about this particular one stayed in my mind. Maybe it was because the roof was blue when nearly all of them are red. Or maybe it was the checkered flags that looked like they'd been torn from my grandmother's tablecloth. It was nothing to comment about, nothing I could explain. It just registered in my mind.

**pronounced bechak*

I said nothing as we passed the old building and stepped up our pace to cross the intersection. Steve pointed ahead and we swung the bikes to the left at the next street. We passed the hospital and the high school and skirted the downtown area. We rode on to the edge of town and passed a well-kept church building with a courtyard and several out-buildings around it.

"That's the church we go to," Steve shouted over his shoulder. The sign said *Gereja Kristen Indonesia.* "Those other buildings round it are the kindergarten and school. I went there to kindergarten for a year."

"We'd better head back," Steve said after a few more minutes. "It's nearly dark now and supper'll be ready."

The night air was cool and lights were beginning to glow in the windows of the houses and shops as we passed. The deserted army camp was coming up now just ahead. We were nearly home. Suddenly Steve slowed his bike and pointed.

"Look over there. Does it look to you like there's a light on in that old place?"

I wasn't sure. "Maybe it's just the way the last rays of sun are hitting it," I told him. "Just reflected off the window."

But as I rode by slowly I looked again. "Hey, you're right. It is a light coming from the bottom window on the right. But so what?"

"So that building hasn't been used for years, that's what," Steve answered. "Why would anybody be in there?"

"Want to take a look?" I asked him.

"Nah, we'd better not. Mom'll worry about us if we're late. Doesn't matter anyway. I was just curious, that's all. That *becak* was going down there... It's strange..." he said, shaking his head.

"Well, maybe they're going to fix it up and use it again," I suggested. "It's only an old wreck of a building anyway, not worth breaking into, so it can't be anything important."

By the time we sat down to supper it was quite cool and a breeze had begun to stir the leaves.

"No rain today," Aunt Lori commented, "but we'll probably get some tomorrow. There's rarely a day goes by without it during this season. Of course in the winter, it's dry all the time and cooler. That's really the beautiful time of the year."

"I hope you get to meet Bonar tomorrow, Alan," Uncle Phil said to me. "He's a good fellow, you'll like him. Comes from Sumatra originally, though he came to us after working in Jakarta a while. Actually I've heard of his uncle. He's quite influential in the university in Sumatra. For years the Christian students have wanted a Christian lecturer from overseas on staff there, but an invitation is never given. We foreigners can't just walk in and start work without being officially invited. At that place they are definitely *not* inviting us. It seems Bonar's uncle, Arifin, is opposed to it and he sways all the others so ... the door stays shut."

He poured iced tea all around and then continued. "Mind you, I haven't discussed all this with Bonar; he doesn't know that I know about it. And

I've never met the uncle personally, it's just that his name keeps coming up. He's a problem. But maybe eventually, now that Bonar's a believer, that'll change."

"So, tell us about your work, Phil," Dad said after the plates of tomatoes and cheese and wonderful fresh bread had been around. " Are we going to be able to see any of it?"

"Sure. We can take you to see the university this evening if you feel like it, or tomorrow. I'm teaching physics right now and also responsible for the *Perkantas* group. That's the student Christian fellowship."

The plate of pale Dutch cheese and crispy bread came by again and I couldn't let it go by for nothing. I lifted a couple more big slices onto my plate. I noticed Debbie did too, in spite of her pretense at dieting.

"Then, as you know, we're involved with the church, too," Uncle Phil was saying. "I do my share of visitation and counseling and so on, and preach when my turn comes. They have three pastors; my job is mostly advising when I'm asked and giving encouragement. This past few months, for instance, I've been trying to develop a better system for teaching all the new candidates for baptism. Something a bit more thorough."

"Sounds like it's a big church," Dad said.

"Fifteen hundred or so. Most of the churches in Indonesia are big. And well educated."

"If the churches are that good, what do they need missionaries for?" I knew it didn't sound very nice, but I couldn't help wondering. I thought missionaries went to places they didn't have many Christians.

Uncle Phil laughed. "We've asked ourselves that too, sometimes, Alan. But the truth is, there's still a need for us. Here, have some more." He passed the plate back my way. "Not everyone in these big congregations is really a child of God. Some are just Christians officially, for the sake of the government records, as it were. Others really believe but have very little solid teaching as a basis for their faith. So there's plenty of room for us."

I took another thick slice of bread. It was warm and the butter oozed into it. Delicious stuff!

"What about you, Lori? I know you've been teaching a little," Mom asked. She'd obviously kept up with their letters better than I had.

"I've taught music for several terms. That's my main job. And quite often I have opportunities for counseling the students too. But recently I've also been working with the Sunday School in upgrading the teaching."

The conversation probably could have continued all night but we were all so tired it began to deteriorate to a series of grunts and yawns. "Go on to bed, Ken," Uncle Phil told Dad. "You make me tired just looking at you! Why don't we save all the activities for tomorrow."

Didn't take us long to agree to that offer. I flopped onto bed that night exhausted. Now I knew what "jet lag" felt like. But much as my body rejoiced at the chance to stretch out, my mind kept racing over the day's events. I closed my eyes to see pictures of a man with a snakeskin briefcase, a would-be thief on a bike and airplanes, airplanes, airplanes. I still wondered why that boy dropped that bag so quickly.

CHAPTER

THREE

When I got up the next morning, there was minor chaos. Mom was so distraught she was almost in tears and kept saying, "I should have known." Aunt Lori was trying to console her and Dad and Uncle Phil were talking. Debbie was standing there in shorts, her long hair uncombed just as she got out of bed, rubbing her eyes and whining.

Mom looked up at me. "Alan, your father's passport's gone. They're all here but his. It must have been stolen. I guess it was in Jakarta when that boy grabbed my bag."

Now I understood her alarm. This was serious. "Are you sure, Mom? You know how you sometimes lose your keys, even though they're in your purse all the time. Maybe you just can't put your fingers on it."

"No, it's gone. Your Dad looked too. They were all here together in this folder. He took that one and

left the rest."

"No wonder he threw away the bag. He didn't want anything else, just the passport. He knew what he was after."

"They're very skillful," Aunt Lori said. "They can get a passport without any problem at all and you'd never know it."

"Why? Doesn't seem like it'd do them any good."

"A passport is worth as much as ten thousand dollars on the streets of Jakarta these days."

"Ten thousand dollars! Wow! That would make them prime targets for theft, wouldn't it."

"What would they want it for?" Debbie asked.

"They can change it and sell it to someone who's .willing to pay for a foreign passport – especially an American one. It's very tricky to make the changes, of course, but it can be done so it looks official. The government is very concerned about cracking down on such thefts, but it's easier said than done."

"The first thing to do is report it to the police, of course," Uncle Phil said decisively. "Then we'll go to Semarang and report it to immigration and get things rolling there to replace it or whatever they have to do."

"Then let's go. Enough time's been wasted as is."

By the time we were ready to leave Mom was looking forward to it. After all, we were doing all we could about the passport. All we could do now was wait, and in the meantime we might as well continue sightseeing. "I have such happy memories of Semarang," she said. "I wanted you to see it anyway, so this will give us a good excuse."

The central part of the island of Java is beautiful. I couldn't get over the view out the car window. Bright green rice fields staggered in terraces up the evenly sloping sides of ancient volcanoes. Off to the left a man trudged steadily behind his water buffalo, ankle deep in mud.

"Are all these mountains volcanic?"

"Nearly all."

"Are they likely to explode any time?"

"They might. Lots of them are inactive, but several in this area are still alive. They erupt every few years. In fact Indonesia has over one hundred volcanoes that are still active."

We turned a corner, swerving to miss a cumbersome ox-cart plodding its way along with a load of wood. "More often, though," Uncle Phil continued, "they just keep bubbling up gently all the time. Like a pot simmering. Never really boiling over." He honked at a flock of geese that decided to wander across the road just then.

"You see that mountain there with a little cloud of steam over it? That's Mount Merbabu. It's like that, just steaming gently all the time. Never really explodes."

A crowded bus rushed past us, almost running into a car coming the other way. Horns honked, brakes squealed and the traffic rushed on. Roads were always crowded here, it seemed. There were the usual cars and buses and trucks, of course. Too many of them. But also the *becaks* and small closed-in vans used as buses, horse-drawn carts called *dokars* and people walking or riding bikes or motorbikes. No wonder the missionaries ask us to pray for safety when they travel.

We rounded a bend and began the long slow hill down into Semarang. From the top of the hill, the reddish-brown tiled roofs below stretched out to the ocean behind them, hazy in the afternoon sun. Semarang's a busy seaport city, the capital of Central Java province. Some of the buildings were built by the Dutch over two hundred years ago, Uncle Phil told us. But it had modern offices and shopping centers too, and more being built everywhere.

While Dad was busy with the immigration officer I walked around the airconditioned office and watched the activities. All the men wore uniforms. Crisp, starched, spotless uniforms. I don't know how they keep looking so neat in this weather. Anyway, there was a pile of brochures lying on the desk, obviously put there for people to take, so I took one.

"What does this mean?" I asked Aunt Lori, pointing to the lettering at the top.

"It's a picture of some of the men most wanted by the immigration department. This one's here on an illegal visa, for instance. This one and this one are on forged passports." I folded the paper and stuck it in my pocket as we left, thinking no more about it.

We stopped in an old restaurant with the front open to the sidewalk and overhead fans doing their best to make an impact on the heat. They helped too, must have been 20 degrees cooler in there than

outside. We ordered pop and rested a bit. Then
Mom and Debbie went off to do some shopping and
the rest of us went looking around. When we got
home again it was about three o'clock.

"Now we've got time to show you the Christian
university where we work," Uncle Phil said. We
pulled into the tree-lined driveway flanked by
bushes of red flowers, and parked the McDonalds'
Toyota. *Nice place,* I thought. Modern concrete
buildings. As good a campus as you'd see anywhere.
A student was working at the reception desk when
we entered the main building.

"This is David," Uncle Phil introduced us to the
serious looking young man with glasses falling
down on his nose. "David works for the school part
time as well as finishing his studies here – right?"

David smiled stiffly in reply. "Yes, I do odd jobs."

He seemed uncomfortable, I thought. He pushed
his glasses up nervously and smiled again, almost
like it was time for another attempt at friendliness.
I noticed the big gold watch that hung on his skinny
arm was too loose.

"David helps in the office and with immigration
red tape — that sort of thing. He's very helpful,"
Uncle Phil put in quickly. "Haven't seen you at
Perkantas lately, David," he added. "Why don't you
come with the group to Borobodur Thursday?"

David smiled weakly but seemed evasive. Probably nervous at being introduced to us foreigners, I
figured. "No, no, thank you. Sometime, sometime.
Thank you. Cannot come this week."

We moved on to tour the offices and classrooms.

"That young man has so much potential I really want to see him make his life count," Uncle Phil commented. "I've spent a lot of hours with him over the past couple years but I still don't know just what's going on with him."

Just then a student came hurrying down the hall toward us and grabbed Uncle Phil's hand, shaking it vigorously. His face seemed to melt away into one huge smile, showing perfect white teeth.

"This is Yakob," my uncle said. "Jacob in English. Yakob's the president of *Perkantas.*"

We shook hands all round and talked for a few minutes. Then Yakob turned to me and said, "You come with us Thursday, OK?"

"Where? I mean, I guess so. Are we?" I looked helplessly at Steve for an explanation.

"Sure, we're planning on it. *Terima kasih,*" he said to Yakob. That was one phrase I knew. It meant "thank you".

Then he said to me, "The *Perkantas* group is going on a trip for the day to Borobodur and we're going with them. That's one of the things I haven't had time to tell you yet."

It was cooler outside after supper. Steve and Debbie and I went out to the back yard.

"Hey, Bonar," Steve called. "Come and meet some cousins of mine from America."

Bonar's room was in one wing of the house, opening onto the yard. He came out, smiling, his neatly combed black hair still wet after his late afternoon bath. He was pulling on an Adidas T-shirt over his shorts.

We played "bola-basket" for a while – that word is so much like English that I latched onto it right away. One more word added to my three word vocabulary! Bonar was good — better than I was. After a while he invited us into the room he shared with a late arriving university student who hadn't been able to find anywhere else to live. His school uniform hung neatly on a hanger for the next day – tan pants and white shirt with a crest on the pocket. On his wall beside the Coca Cola calendar were three pictures. One of a man I recognized as Indonesia's president, the second a postcard of a lake and mountains and some kind of house with a roof that tipped up on the ends like horns.

"That is a picture of Sumatra," Bonar explained. "I come from Sumatra; it's very beautiful."

"Sumatra. That's the big island to the northwest of here, right?" I had a picture of the country mapped in my mind, thanks to my mom's coaching. "And who is this?" I asked about the third picture. It was just a snapshot tacked with a thumbtack. All I could see was a thin-faced man in a white shirt with a heavy head of hair. Along the bottom in handwriting was the name, T R Arifin.

"My uncle. His name is Arifin. When my father died I went to live with my uncle; he is a teacher in university. Has lots of money, and nice house. Travels a lot, to Singapore, Taiwan, Philippines, even to America and twice to Holland. He has little business he works on at night and want me to work with him, but I don't want to. We don't .. how you say it, don't be so friendly together."

"Don't get along very well," Steve helped. Bonar nodded and continued, "Then he was in little bit of trouble. Police came to our house. I don't know what was going on but he and my aunt had big fight. I decided I would get out. So I left and came to capital city, Jakarta. My uncle would not be happy if he knew I am now a Christian." He flashed an intensely white smile as he said this and added, "Maybe some day I will tell him."

We wandered back out into the yard as we talked. We were standing by the banana palms over against the fence when the trees across the fence began to swing. I looked up just as a yellowish-gray silky body appeared and next thing I knew, onto the fence dropped a monkey. It sat there observing us for a second. I noticed his face was pale and smooth compared to the darker hair which stood up on top of his head.

"That's the army monkey. He's a pet at the army camp just up the road. He wanders over quite often."

I got a bit nearer. It isn't usual to have real monkeys swinging onto your back fence in Milwaukee. I was wishing he'd come closer.

"Don't touch," Bonar warned. "They can bite."

"Yeah," Steve agreed. "If you don't watch he'll take things too." It must have been his cue. Just as he finished the sentence, the monkey reached out one long arm and took the comb right out of my pocket. It was so fast I hardly knew what happened. Before I could react he shinnied back up the tree, swung over the fence and was gone. So much for that comb.

"What kind of monkey was that? Wow! What a thief!" I said to Steve.

"He's a macaque. They're native to Sumatra. Real smart too. Those guys have been employed by the Forestry Department of Malaysia to collect flowers and coconuts. They know which ones are ripe and which aren't."

Just what we need – a monkey with an award for academic excellence.

"Hey, do you suppose it was a monkey like that that stole my Dad's passport? If they're so trainable and can steal that fast..."

"Uh-uh." Steve was shaking his head. "What stole your dad's passport was not a monkey, I'm afraid. It was a very ordinary human being. Monkeys might be smart but they aren't influenced by the $10,000 a passport will bring. People, however, are."

"Yeah, no question about that."

When I took off my shorts to go to bed that night, I absent-mindedly stuck my hand in the pocket. There was the folded piece of paper I'd picked up in Semarang. It was too hot to sleep for a while anyway, and Steve was reading. So I unfolded the paper, grabbed a pencil off the table and began to doodle. I've always been one for doodling and coming up with cartoons. I drew mustaches and crazy ears and colored in glasses where there were none on the faces staring up at me from the page. Suddenly I realized something.

"That looks just like him! Steve," I said suddenly. "I saw this guy. Here, this one. Look at him. I saw him. He was having some trouble with the police in the airport in Jakarta when we arrived. I noticed him in his dark glasses. When I put glasses on this picture, it's his face! He's here in Indonesia – I saw him arrive. I wonder how long it'll take the immigration department to discover his whereabouts and catch him."

"Depends," Steve answered without enthusiasm. He was too caught up in reading some sci-fi book to pay much attention. But I knew I was right about the man in the dark glasses. And I felt maybe there was something bigger going on here. Or was I just being over-dramatic again? Probably. I crumpled the paper up in a tight little wad and threw it in the waste basket.

CHAPTER

FOUR

Steve knew as soon as he woke up that he was sick. His mom said he had a fever and should stay in bed. He didn't look like he wanted to do anything else anyway so I guess that suited him just fine.

"Bonar's off school today, though," Aunt Lori told me. "You and he can do something together, I'm sure."

We shot a few baskets, and had stopped for a drink of juice when my aunt called us.

"Would you boys like to do something for me? I need some brown sugar and I hate to ask the cook to stop her work and go get it. Anyway it would be fun for you, Alan, to see the market." She said something to Bonar in Indonesian and gave him some money, then we were off on our bikes.

At least we would be if there had been any place to fit a bike wheel between all the other things occupying the road. Bonar wove his way calmly between cars, motorbikes and *becaks,* narrowly missing an oncoming semi-trailer. I tried to follow.

"Hey, Bonar, hold on, will you. I'm not used to risking my life everytime I want to go to the store! This traffic is wild!"

He grinned and pulled over to the shoulder, taking advantage of a gap in the traffic flow.

"Never mind. We are nearly there. The market." He pointed straight ahead to a series of long roofed shelters. We moved on and chained our bikes to a post outside one of the buildings. So this was an Asian market I'd heard Mom talk about.

To my left a man sold birds in bamboo cages of various sizes and styles. As I was looking at them I almost walked into a lady squatting by a little charcoal fire baking some kind of cake things; a man on the right just behind her had all kinds of belts hanging on a rack and spread out on the table. A voice behind me called, in English, "Hats, hats!" and I looked to see a young man with an assortment of headgear hanging on hooks. "Five hundred, five hundred," he said, grinning as I passed. Probably that was the price, I thought. I didn't dare stop or I'd lose Bonar.

We stepped under the shade of a roof now. I wanted to stand still a minute and take it all in. Long rows of booths sold everything; I mean everything. Each seller had a few square feet of space and they made the most of it.

A lot of them seemed to have cloth material or some kinds of clothes. Most of it was the Indonesian specialty called batik that I knew my mom would like. One stall sold bits and pieces – combs, toothpaste, writing paper, matches – you name it. Sort of like a Handi-Mart or Family Drugs store condensed into three feet. We passed along the rows. Leatherwork, jewelry, papers, and magazines, medicines, paintings, on and on. I began to notice things repeating and after a while everything sort of looked alike.

But suddenly we came to the end and turned a corner to the food part. As we walked past delicious looking bread I stopped and took a big whiff. Mmm! one good thing for sure came from the Dutch period in Indonesia – they left their bread recipes. I'd never seen such a variety of delicious, hot-from-the-oven breads. Then there was fruit, vegetables, noodles and rice, sauces and bottles and cans I couldn't identify. I didn't want to ask Bonar about everything but there were lots of things I hadn't seen before. Then we came to the meat.

"Look out," Bonar shouted to me. A man staggered in bent under the carcass of a cow. He heaved it up on a table, wiped his forehead and went back for another one. Two men in grungy T-shirts hacked large chunks of red meat from the carcasses the haulers carried in. I watched a lady pick out a piece. She seemed to be talking a lot about it – I guessed the price was too high – then the seller added another chunk to the meat already on the scales. The lady seemed satisfied so the seller wrapped it neatly in a huge dark banana leaf, pinnned it with a kind of toothpick and took her money. I was surprised at the whole procedure. It would hardly pass inspection in a supermarket at home yet it

seemed to be acceptable even to this well-dressed,
immaculately clean lady who looked like she would
never tolerate dirt in her own home.

Just beside the produce was the ready-to-eat
stuff. I caught the aroma of garlic frying in the
shallow metal frying pans called *woks*. When the
oil was nice and hot the cook dropped in whatever
they were cooking and it sizzled and sputtered to a
golden brown. Mmm. My stomach growled. It looked
good – especially the shrimp and bite-size bits of
chicken. The aroma trailed me temptingly as I
followed Bonar down the aisle.

He was at a stall selling flour, sugar, corn starch,
canned milk and so on. Plastic bags of sugar sat on
the counter and a huge burlap sack of peanuts
stood open behind it. I saw Bonar point at some
round chunks of brown solid substance. *"Gula
merah,"* he said to the seller who reached for a piece
and weighed it. It seemed this was too big a piece
because Bonar said something else and the lady
broke off a chunk about as big as a coffee mug and
wrapped it in a plastic bag.

"Is that brown sugar?"

"Yes. Have a piece – very sweet." We broke off
little pea-sized bits of the hard stuff and popped it
in our mouths. It was delicious – almost like the
maple sugar candy we get in Wisconsin.

We looked a little longer and then headed for our
bikes. The hat salesman was still trying to sell caps
– everything from LA Rams baseball caps to Mickey
Mouse "ears". I heard him say, "You want hat,
boy?" as we jumped on our bikes and headed out

into the street.

I noticed a camera shop directly across from the market and we went over there before heading home, because I needed some film. Behind the display of Nikkon cameras, plastic beads strung on six-foot strands hung side by side forming a curtain that rippled intriguingly as a man stepped out from the back room and took his place at the counter. He was very friendly and we got talking. He wanted to know where I came from and I told him. Then he asked how long I was going to be in Indonesia, what I was going to see, who I was staying with and so on. He was trying his best to speak English so I was trying to help him with words he didn't know, and I told him I was visiting the McDonalds who teach at the university.

"Oh, yes. Satya Wacana. Yes, I know. He is tall man with beard, right?"

"Yes. You know him then?"

"A little. He comes here for pictures develop. He lives by university?"

"No, he lives on Jalan Lima."

"Jalan Lima. Number five street," the man repeated, translating for himself. "House with white wall."

"Fence. Yes. It has a white fence."

We were doing so well communicating I was really quite pleased with myself, but we couldn't stand and talk all day so we paid for the film and left.

We maneuvered our bikes down a narrow street that was more like a lane really. The small shops on each side didn't seem to be doing much business. A girl about six years old stood jiggling a baby on one hip watching us pass. A couple other kids rode a tricycle, one pedaling and the other riding in a back seat. I noticed plants and bird cages on the balconies above the stores. Miniature botanical gardens seemed to thrive in a space no bigger than my grandma's kitchen table top. Amazing what people can do with such a tiny space. I relaxed a little and we slowed our pedaling and began to enjoy the scenery. Ahead of us was a perfect cone-shaped mountain, as evenly shaped as those in a third-grader's drawing. The red and white Indonesian flag fluttered weakly in front of it.

Then I looked back.

A weird feeling started creeping over me at what I saw. Coming our way, about two blocks behind, was a *becak* with a blue roof. I hoped that was all, but no, there they were – matching blue and white checked flags flapping on antennae at the sides. No doubt about it – it was the same *becak* I'd seen going down the road to the deserted army camp. I knew if I looked at the back I'd see that same ridiculous license plate flopping.

I turned back to my riding. It didn't mean anything, I told myself. The town was swarming with *becaks*. Out of the hundreds it wasn't surprising if one kept popping up where we were. Just coincidence. He probably has a passenger going out this way. Bonar was talking about something and I tried to listen for a while. Then I glanced back again, trying to look casual. It was coming closer now and I saw there was a passenger – a very heavy man wearing a white shirt and black pants. That was all I could tell about him from one quick look.

"Bonar," I interrupted his silence, "Bonar, look behind us. Do you see anything odd about that *becak?* I've seen it before."

He gave a good long look and I was afraid it was too obvious.

"Never mind the *becak*," he answered suddenly. "The passenger. I know that man. Let's get out of here."

CHAPTER

FIVE

I didn't have time to get a look at the man Bonar was so afraid of. He started pedaling furiously and I was close behind him. We rounded the next corner, narrowly missing a motorbike coming the other way, rattled over the bridge, turned down a side street and headed into a little road that led between a bunch of houses.

I was thoroughly lost by this time. I kept Bonar in sight and concentrated strictly on pedaling as fast as I could. It seemed like we were in a sort of housing subdivision. The road twisted and wound randomly between the houses with no landmark that I could notice. Neither of us turned around to see if our pursuer was still behind. We didn't dare.

Finally Bonar pulled onto a bigger road that I recognized as being just a few hundred yards from the McDonalds' house. Was I ever glad to see the place! We circled into the yard with great relief, and I dismounted, legs wobbly from the ordeal.

"Whew! What a ride! Why were we running anyway? Who is the guy?"

"Man I knew once in Jakarta. I don't want to see him."

Bonar turned and went into his room and that seemed to be the end of that.

My mind was whirling but my questions would have to wait. I headed for the house and a cold drink.

"One of the problems with working in Indonesia," Uncle Phil was explaining to Dad when I entered, "is the visa situation. It's hard to get a visa in the first place, for anything more than a visit, and once you get them they have to be renewed annually."

"Why do you have to have visa to live in another country?" Debbie asked. "Won't MasterCharge or some other kind do just as well?"

Uncle Phil laughed. "The visa I'm talking about is not a credit card, Debbie. It's a stamp in your passport that says you have permission to enter the country as a visitor, or to live and work there."

I knew what he was talking about. I think Debbie did too if she had stopped to think.

"Trouble is," Uncle Phil continued, "the process takes so long that by the time you get the new one it's almost half expired."

"So you start applying for next year's right away," Dad said.

"Almost. It's really very time-consuming." He crossed the room and sat down. " But it has to be done if we want to go on living here – and we do.

Anyway, it's just another thing you can pray for for us.

"You met David, the student at the front desk at the university? Well, fortunately he helps us with immigration matters. Does them for the university as a regular thing so it makes it easier and saves us struggling with it all ourselves. He seems very good at dealing with bureaucracy."

I waited for a break in the conversation and then told Dad and Uncle Phil about our chase. "I don't know why Bonar was so scared of the guy. Looked harmless enough to me."

Uncle Phil twisted his mouth thoughtfully and said nothing for a minute. "You never know. We don't know much about Bonar's past. He was living in Jakarta for a while, that much we know. But we didn't ask many questions. Could be that he was in some unsavory activities that Bonar would just as soon forget about now that he's a Christian."

"Like what?"

"Oh, you never know. The life of a boy on the streets in Jakarta can be very hard. Everybody's crowding in to the capital city trying to get work, start a better life. Sometimes the only work to be had is ...well, illegal, or shady to say the least."

"I don't think Bonar would do anything like that."

"Not now he wouldn't. He's given his life to Christ since he came here. Just a few months ago, in fact. It really made a change in him. But it might not be easy for him to stand if he was thrown in with his old friends again. You know how it is, for any of us – it's sometimes easier to be a Christian when we're with people that approve."

Dad smiled. "Sure. That's true in America just as much as here."

"Actually," Uncle Phil went on, "there can be a lot of trouble for a Christian who takes a stand, especially in some areas of the country and in some situations. That's why the tendency often is to just keep quiet. Can I get you some iced tea?"

He returned with two big glasses full of tea and ice cubes.

"We have a lot of name-only Christians, "he continued. "I guess what the church here in Indonesia needs is more 'salt'. Know what I mean?"

"You bet I do. Again, the same could be said for America," Dad replied. "And we have less excuse."

I knew what he was referring to. There's a place in the Bible where Jesus said we are suppposed to be like salt in the world. Just a few grains of salt makes everything around it salty. Suddenly I remembered Josh. He's a top-notch pitcher and we were all glad to have him on the baseball team. He'd given us a nine and six standing at the end of last season. Besides that, he's a nice guy and real popular. Friendly, good looking, and always dressed better than most of us – the kind of guy everyone wants to hang around with. That's why when he suggests anything I don't want to be the one to always object, even if I know his idea isn't right. Like when he suggested we cause trouble in Mr Howard's math class in retaliation for his giving us a pop quiz, I sure wasn't going to say anything. I

knew it wasn't a good idea. Actually I kind of liked
Mr. Howard – I guess that's 'cause I was good in
math. Anyway I knew it was our own fault for not
being prepared for that kind of test. But when Josh
came up with his idea and everybody else agreed...
well, I wasn't going to be the only one to look like a
jerk. There were other times too, if I really thought
about it, when my Christian salt wasn't very salty.

"Anyway, tonight you'll meet some of the cream
of the crop," Uncle Phil went on. "Christian students. We have them over once a month, just for
fellowship. We sing, and they share prayer re-
quests. Very informal. You'll enjoy meeting them,
I know."

When the time came, the students arrived and
made themselves at home. Half of them sat on the
floor, like I did, their bare feet tucked behind them.
Beside me Debbie and a couple students played
guitars, another one, a harmonica. I was impressed
with the music that rolled out naturally from their
voices and fingers. Times like this made me deter-
mine to practice the piano a little more often. I
could feel the music, soft and gentle, like a warm
blanket over me, as they sang song after song.
Descants, tenor, alto... all the parts seemed to ooze
together into one delicious sound. Before long I
found myself joining in a song.

*"Allah-ku baik. Allah-ku baik. Allah-ku baik,
amat baik pada ku."* I knew the chorus in English.
"God is so good, God is so good, God is so good, He's
so good to me."

I was really into the music with my whole body.

I didn't notice until later that Bonar was sitting on the sidelines, barely participating. *What's the matter with him,* I wondered, but my uncle's voice brought me back.

"Let's take a few minutes for prayer," he suggested. "I know some of you have problems, things you need to talk to God about. Let's share these so we can pray for each other."

"Well, I'd like you to pray for me." It was Yakob who spoke first, Bible in hand, his face split by a white-toothed smile. Yakob, I found out, was the oldest of the students in the group. He had become a Christian just three years ago and wanted to be a teacher after graduation.

"I can't afford to be out of work for long; my family will not help me since I became a Christian. So, I'd like you to pray that God will provide the right job, in the place He wants me to teach, whether in a Christian school or a public school. I would like to stay on Java, but I'll go anywhere God directs me."

Several other seniors wanted prayer for jobs. Someone wanted prayer for healing. Another wanted us to pray for her mother who had been sick for years. One or two asked prayer for parents who weren't Christians. Uncle Phil told them about Dad's missing passport and asked them to pray that it would be returned or replaced without delay. I could tell by the reaction of the group that they realized how serious it was to be stuck in a foreign country without any passport. Several prayed and Uncle Phil prayed last.

After they'd gone I said to Steve, "Those guys are really musical. They make me ashamed of myself."

"Yeah, I know what you mean."

"You know, I'm kinda getting to like it here. I can see why you feel at home."

Steve laughed. "It *is* home. The only home I've ever known. In fact I don't like the year we have to spend in the States on home assignment. I never really feel – well, 'in'."

"Don't you miss stuff you can't get here, though?"

"Like what? We get enough. Well, I'll admit, one thing I did enjoy about being in the US was pizza. I would like to be able to go to a pizza place now and then!"

"And you really enjoy Faith Academy, do you?"

Steve shrugged. "School's school. You know what I mean. But Faith's as good as any school at home. We have everything – baseball, basketball, a school paper and yearbook, field trips, a band. In fact one of our own missionaries from Wisconsin is the band director. And there's always friends around to do things with. As schools go, it's a good place."

I really couldn't feel too sorry for him in a place like that. Then I remembered the more immediate situation.

"I wonder what's the matter with Bonar," I said. "When we were in town today the strangest thing happened. That same *becak* we saw going towards the old army camp last night started following us and Bonar saw who was riding in it and took off like a wild man. We gave him the slip I think but I still don't know what for. Said he knew him in Jakarta.

And tonight he seemed sort of out of it when the students were here."

No sooner had I said this than there was a knock at the back door, which was still open, and Bonar's face appeared.

"You are not in bed?"

"No, not yet. Come on in." I wanted to say something to get things rolling because I was dying to ask him about this afternoon. "I enjoyed our visit to the market," I said. "Thanks for taking me."

"Yes. You're welcome."

"You really led a high speed chase coming home, though. Why did we have to outrun that *becak?*"

His dark eyes clouded over and there was an intensity about his voice as he answered, "I know that man. I don't want him to see me."

Might as well take the plunge and ask. "Why, Bonar? What's wrong?"

"I knew him in Jakarta. I... I worked for him. It was... not honest. I don't want to talk about it. But when he knows I am here he will want to take me back again or something. I could be in trouble."

"Well, we got away from him, so don't worry."

"Yes, but he can find out where I live. You told."

"Told who?" Then I remembered the camera shop conversation. "You mean that man in the shop? What's he got to do with it?"

"Don't you see? The man who followed us came out of that shop. He was probably in there when you were talking. He will have heard it all. Now he can find me."

I remembered the beaded curtain behind the

counter. "You mean that fat guy was in the back room all the time we were talking, listening to the whole conversation?"

"Yes. Then he followed us."

I still wasn't clear on his reasoning but I could see he was really scared. "I'm sorry. I had no idea." I thought to myself that Bonar would have the advantage over the man anyway, because the other man was so overweight. But I didn't say so.

"No, it's not your fault. I didn't know at the time either, until I saw the man follow us from there. Then I know. Too late now." Then he shrugged his shoulders and changed the subject. We talked a few minutes about other things and he left.

What could I make of all the little bits of mystery that had popped up here and there since I arrived? I tried to piece it together. A man at the airport who seems to be wanted for some kind of immigration violation. My dad's passport missing. A silly looking *becak* going to a supposedly deserted building. And a fat man from Bonar's mysterious past chasing us in that same *becak* because of an address I gave unknowingly to the camera store salesman. It didn't add up to much. But I could feel my detective senses rising quickly.

CHAPTER

SIX

"What d'you know about Borobodur?" Steve asked me the next morning as we filled our canteens with water to take with us. The university Christian fellowship group were leaving about nine and Yakob had promised to pick us up and take us along.

"Nothing," I told him. "I guess it wasn't here in Mom's day – she's never mentioned it."

Steve laughed. "Oh, it was here all right. Unless your Mom's over twelve hundred years old!"

"Not quite. Twelve hundred years!"

"Yup. It was built about 800 AD. Neglected and buried from ten hundred or so till the nineteenth century. Now it's being restored so it won't fall apart." A honk told us the students were here for us. We climbed into the airconditioned van. "What is Borobodur anyway?" I asked as we got rolling. "Is it a building?"

"Well, not exactly. It's kind of like the pyramids

in a way. You walk up stairs and round and round, up and up five levels to the very top. You don't go *in* it; you go *on* it."

"Is it a temple or a tomb or what?"

"It's the world's largest Buddhist monument. I guess you'd call it a temple. I can't describe it. You'll see when we get there."

When we finally arrived, the driver chose a parking place. The lot was almost full. I could see we weren't the only ones touring Borobodur that day.

"This place is always crowded," Steve said.

"Isn't every place? I haven't seen an empty spot since we arrived on this island."

"Yeah, I guess so. I don't think about it anymore but Java *is* supposed to be the most crowded spot on earth. I believe it when I come here. Look at the crowds."

We joined them and walked the direction everyone else was walking, up the road past souvenir stalls and into the east gate. I began to get a good look at the structure.

"Man! this thing's big."

"Yeah, I think it's 105 feet high," Steve said.

My first impression was that it wasn't smooth like I'd imagined but seemed to be a mass of humps, bumps, turrets, and spires. When I got closer I saw it was actually covered completely in carvings. The stone was discolored and some was worn away or covered with moss and junk but you could easily see the figures carved in it. Each rock, say, maybe a piece of arm or leg, fitted in with others to make a whole picture.

"This thing's like one mega-jigsaw puzzle!" I said to Steve.

"Yeah. You can imagine how much fun the engineers are having taking it apart piece by piece to clean it and put slabs under it and then putting it all back together again!"

"Is that what the cranes are doing here?"

"Yes. They've been working on it for years, but it's nearly done. I think all the pictures tell stories from the life of Buddha."

It was hard for me to make any sense out of all the rows and rows of carvings. "About the only thing I can see for sure is that it took a lot of work to make this."

"About eighty years actually."

"How many other facts do you know? You're always coming out with a new bit of information. You sound like a history teacher."

"I know all this because I read about it a few months ago and decided to do a report on it for school."

After a while Bonar and Steve went over to talk to Yakob about something. I was looking around and said I'd meet them in a few minutes. That's when I saw something that caught my eye. At the very top level, a few steps above me, were stone *stupas,* giant bell-shaped things with statues of Buddha inside them. There was more open space up there and no walls around it like on the lower levels. A few yards away, beside one of the stupas, was a snakeskin briefcase and two men standing talking. Where had I seen that briefcase before? I knew I recognized it from somewhere.

I climbed a few steps to that upper level and walked casually toward one of the stupas. I could see the men well now without being seen. One of them I recognized instantly from his size. It was the man in the blue-roofed *becak*! For some reason Bonar's former boss was making some kind of deal with the owner of the briefcase. As the sun caught the gold initials "TRA", a scene in the airport came back to my mind. And now I recognized that man too. His eyes were hidden by sunglasses but his cheek had a wart.

Icy chills crept over me in spite of the weather.

I ran my hands over the stone and put them through the holes in the rocks like others were doing, trying to look like a normal tourist. People came and went, not paying attention to me at all. Just what I wanted, so I could keep an eye on my two "suspects".

"Suspected" of what, I wasn't sure. I was curious though. More than curious maybe. They were deep in serious conversation and I saw the owner of the briefcase, Mr TRA, hand a package to the fat man. A large brown envelope. Then in a few minutes they broke up and each melted into the crowd and disappeared.

Well, so much for that, I told myself. *If there's anything going on, you'll never know now.*

It was about half an hour later that I saw them again. Yakob and I were watching a group of Japanese tourists posing and re-posing for pictures which they snapped constantly. I happened to look off to one side and there at the back gate was the overweight stranger, the man with the briefcase and another man getting into a car together. As the third man bent over to get in the door I couldn't see his face, but one side of his head was toward me and I saw he had one ear missing. Well, it wasn't exactly missing. It was more deformed, only a little curly stub of cartilage which should have been an ear and wasn't. I guess he was born that way. Anyway I got one good look at him before he climbed in the car with the other two and rode off.

Whoa! What was going on here? Not that it had anything to do with me. I was only a visitor. But I just couldn't resist a good bit of mystery. Sort of like seeing a police car chasing down the street, lights flashing, siren blaring. You know it's none of your business but you can't help wondering what he's after. I guess this was kind of the same thing.

Somehow I was going to figure this out, at least enough to put my curiosity to rest. But for now I'd better not lose Yakob. I hurried to catch up. It was getting harder and harder to convince myself that the businessmen were none of my affair.

CHAPTER

W e had started back to the van when Bonar
poked me and pointed to a crowd off to the right.

"Look. They watch a show. Let's look."

I caught a glimpse of a man in the center who
seemed to be doing tricks or something. We joined
the crowd for a closer look. It turned out to be a man
with a trained dog on a leash and a monkey in a
white cage. When I joined the crowd and elbowed
my way in so I could see, the monkey was on the
dog's back riding him like a horse. After riding in a
little circle, the monkey jumped off and clapped his
hands, applauding his own act.

Then it was the dog's turn. He jumped through
a hoop the man held. Back and forth two or three
times. Then the two animals danced together. The
Indonesian kids all around me were really enjoying
it. I have to admit it was pretty good, especially
when I think of how hard it was for me to train my
terrier, Ivory, to even "sit" or "stay". I tried for

months with that dumb dog. Finally I got her to
obey about two-thirds of the time, so I quit.

Anyway by now the act was over and people were
throwing money into the little cup the monkey was
holding. As the crowd broke up Bonar and I ran to
join the rest of the bunch who were getting in the
van.

"Wow! Those monkeys are smart. It'd be fun to
have one for a pet," I said to Steve as we headed
home.

"Yes, they are. That was another macaque. I've
read where people have even trained monkeys like
that to dress themselves, and to play a piano!"

"What if I took one back to Wisconsin!"

"What about a gibbon?" Debbie put in. "I'd like a
gibbon. They just wrap those long arms around you
and hang on. I knew a man once..."

"Uh-uh," Steve said. "You don't want one of
those. Gibbons don't make good pets. They don't
like to be kept inside, for one thing, and they're too
vicious to leave unchained."

"They bite," Bonar put in. "Hard. And sometimes
have even attacked people."

"Yes, and you know what? Gibbons can't swim.
Their long hair gets waterlogged and they drown,"
Steve added. "Bet ya didn't know that. It's true. I
read that in an encyclopedia," he said, defending
himself. Debbie looked skeptical.

"Changing the subject," Yakob said from the
front seat, "what did you think of Borobodur, Alan?"

"It's awesome. Huge." Debbie and I seemed to
agree for once.

"All those carvings! I don't see how anybody can take time to do all that detailed carving."

"What does it all mean anyhow?"

"Seems to be based on old legends of Buddha's life or something."

Yakob was saying "...is a Buddhist monument. Of course most Indonesians are not Buddhist. They are Muslim – they follow the religion of Islam. They don't have any statues or monuments because they don't believe in idols."

I remembered hearing something about Islam in church a while ago. I said to Yakob, "They follow Mohammed, right?"

"Yes. They believe Mohammed has the truth about God and they follow his teachings in a book called the Koran."

He turned suddenly to the left to avoid a hole in the road and swung back again just in time to miss a truck.

"Muslims believe they have to do certain things to get God's blessing: pray five times a day, and go without eating during the daytime once a year for a month. That's called the Fast of Ramadan," he continued.

The students around were all talking in Indonesian as we carried on our conversation in English. Eventually, Steve said, "Officially, there's no opposition to Christianity here. The constitution makes it perfectly legal to be a Christian. There's a lot of freedom really. They have Christian programs on TV, and if there's enough kids from Christian families in a school, they actually have to study

Christianity in religious instruction classes. We
even have a missionary friend that helps write the
lessons."

"That's great. Sounds better than in the US."

"Well, not really, because in the west people
have so many things to help them."

"Like what?"

"Like Christian books and magazines, for one
thing. Sunday School lessons and work books and
all that stuff, films, summer camp and conferences,
even Christian music. Indonesia has some of course,
but not nearly as much and it's more expensive
than it is in the States."

"Yeah, I see what you mean. I guess you're right.
We do have it easier." I thought of Bonar and how
he seemed to be afraid of his uncle knowing he'd
become a Christian. I couldn't imagine anyone in
my family ever being mad at me for being a Christian. In fact I didn't know what I'd do if I ever met
that kind of reaction.

On the ride home we passed more of the beautiful, evenly shaped mountains I'd seen on the way to
Semarang. In some places orangey-red lilies were
blooming against the bright green rice fields,
making it even more appealing. I felt like I was
standing in the middle of a postcard.

"Hey, Bonar, we've got a while yet before we get
home. How 'bout teaching me some Indonesian? I
can say thank you – *terima kasih* – and I learned
bola-basket the first five minutes that I knew you.
But teach me something else."

"OK. You should learn to count. One, two, three,

like this: *satu, dua, tiga, empat, lima, enam...*"

"Whoa! Wait a minute. Not all at once." I copied him as closely as I could.

"Good. Now we test." Bonar was grinning widely as he tried to think up a phrase for me to use. "*Anjing* is dog. *Anjing*. Easy. Now say 'three dogs'."

"*Tiga anjings*".

Bonar and Steve laughed. "Not *anjings*; just *anjing*. Don't add an s. It doesn't matter if there's one or a bunch of something. But you're right otherwise. *Tiga anjing*."

"Now try 'two basketballs'."

I thought for a minute. *Satu, dua*, yes, that was it. "*Dua bola-basket*."

Everyone cheered and laughed and the university students got into the act now too. All the rest of the way home they had great fun trying to put a few more Indonesian words into my head.

It was raining when Yakob left us off at the house. We ran inside, mud spattering our legs, raced for the shower and cleaned up for supper. The rain continued all evening, filling up the ditches and pouring off the road. A newspaper and an old tin can, picked up by the wind, went skating across the road. Branches were ripped from the smaller trees. Ditches that were dug extra deep to carry all the water quickly filled and overflowed. Lightning ripped through the sky. After every flash the rain seemed to pound even harder. The tin roof over the kitchen area magnified the sound to a deafening roar. Even in the rest of the house with its tile roof the steady drumming pounded on our ears, loud, heavy, pausing only for another roll of thunder and then returning to drum again.

Looking out the window was like standing under a waterfall, watching a steady sheet of water pour down in front of your face. I didn't know it was possible for it to rain so much. It was worth it, though, for the coolness the winds brought. In fact, it was almost chilly. I felt more energetic than I had since we'd arrived. Energetic enough to play a game of Monopoly with Debbie and Steve. Bonar probably would have played with us too, but he had gone straight to his room and was settled in, warm and dry for the night.

"I'm sure not going to ask him to come out on a night like this," Steve said. That's when I suddenly realized something. I'd completely forgotten to tell Bonar about the men I had seen at Borobodur, one of whom I knew was his former boss. Bonar might have been able to help figure out what was going on. Who was the one with the shades and the briefcase? What were they doing anyway?

"Hey, Alan, it's your turn. What's the matter, you're not paying attention."

"Huh? Oh, yeah, sure I am. Here I go. Watch me land on Park Place."

CHAPTER

EIGHT

After the rain, the bright cool morning that greeted us was a royal treat. In fact, it stayed relatively cool all day and even looked like it might rain again as Bonar and Steve and I sat under a tree in the back yard later that afternoon looking at Steve's collection of airplane models. He had rounded them up from every corner of his room and brought them outside.

He had everything from a model of the Kitty Hawk to the latest stealth bomber, with biplanes, experimental aircraft, jumbo jets and everything in between.

One of the models had a rotor that wouldn't turn.

"When I stuck it down, I got glue over here where I shouldn't have," he explained, "and now the whole rotating bit is stuck in place."

"If we could scrape the glue off just here, see, where it's... Hey, I can fix it."

I pulled out my Swiss Army knife and began to

scrape carefully away on the glue blob. Here was a good chance to prove the usefulness of my knife.

"Hey, look at that knife!" Steve said admiringly. "Look how many blades it has. What can it do?"

"All sorts of things. See, it has a corkscrew, a tiny blade and a great big one..." I pulled out each blade cautiously, letting the wonders of each one sink in. "Even a saw. This little saw blade can actually cut down a tree."

"Aw, c'mon. Cut down a tree?"

"A small one." I justified my words. "It really can, I've seen it done. One man I saw cut down a sapling about an inch and a half around with one of these."

My audience was duly impressed, I could see.

We worked a bit more and I loaned Bonar my knife for a minute to scrape a little while I worked on another plane. He finished scraping, laid the knife down beside him on the grass and tried to turn the blades with his fingers.

"Hey, I think you've got it," Steve said. "Thanks a lot. Let's see if it'll turn just by blowing on it like it should."

Debbie came out to watch us and to admire Steve's planes – or Steve, I'm not sure which. She stood beside him, oohing and aahing over all his models as if she knew something about them.

Just then a movement on the fence beside us made us all look up. Our friend, the army monkey, was sitting there, grinning at us.

"Oh, so you're back," Steve said to it. "What are you after this time, you pilfering little long-armed crook?"

In an instant we had our answer to that. The monkey jumped down to within a few feet of us, then before we could blink, he darted over to the knife, grabbed it in one paw and was gone.

"Hey!" I jumped to my feet but he was up on the fence now and off to the other side. I scrambled up behind him. There were trees all around and I could see it wouldn't do me any good to run after him. The monkey was out of sight and with him went my knife.

I was really mad. "Wow, what a thief! If these monkeys are so smart I hope he knows how to bring my knife back." After I had calmed down a bit I said, "Actually, if he's as smart as you say, he'll probably sell it and retire on the profits. Those things are expensive!"

"We can chase him," Bonar suddenly suggested. "On bike. I know where he will go – back to the old army camp. If he drops it there we can get it back. Let's go."

"Not much chance," Steve said. "Besides I've got other things to do right now. You guys go on. I have to grab a snack and go out with Mom to get some shopping done for school. We should be home by supper. See you later."

"Good luck," Debbie said, waving as Bonar and I pulled out.

We crossed the railway tracks and turned down the gravel road to the left where we had seen the *becak* going on our previous ride.

"D'you think it's all right? Snooping around an army camp, I mean."

"Sure. Nobody uses it now. It's empty. We can at least look around the outside. He might have dropped the knife somewhere."

I was at the gate now and it swung open easily. We parked our bikes just inside the gate and looked around. Besides the two main buildings there was an old well, covered over now, a couple of sheds, an out-of-order jeep and a rusting tank parked under a metal roof.

Bonar climbed up into the seat of the old tank. "Hey, look, this gun still turns," he said, grabbing the control stick. We found some levers and buttons and things and we fooled around for a while. It was a neat place and we probably spent longer than it seemed. The sky was getting quite overcast by now. I kept my eyes on the alert for a red army knife but I didn't see anything. We climbed out of the tank and investigated some other things and then out of nowhere came a swishing sound in the tree above me and down at my feet landed the monkey.

"Hey, here's our thief. Wonder if he can show us where he dropped my knife."

For a minute the monkey stood there in front of me, screeching and showing his dirty white teeth. I didn't move. Those yellowed molars could damage a leg in no time and maybe even give me rabies. I waited. Then for no apparent reason he turned and ran off to the front of the nearest big building, jumped up on a ledge and pushed his way inside through a broken window.

I was after him. "Stop! Hey!" I yelled, chasing him. Bonar was right behind me. We ran toward

the main door. It was closed as I expected it to be.
What I hadn't expected though was the shiny lock
hooked through the metal bolt. I stopped dead in
my tracks.

"Bonar, look at this," I said. "This lock looks new.
That's funny."

Bonar looked over my shoulder. "I wonder why
they would lock up this old place," I said.

" They wouldn't lock a building unless there's
something inside," Bonar agreed. "Alan, d'you think
there's something – valuable – maybe in here?" I
could feel the goose bumps rising on my arm as he
asked the question.

"I don't know. But we've got to get my knife from
that ape. C'mon, we'll find another way in."

"But Alan..." I guess he was going to object to
breaking and entering, but I wasn't listening. I was
determined to chase that monkey till I found my
knife. He ran after me and circled the building a
different way. In a minute I heard him calling me
from around the corner.

"Come, Alan, here is a way in. Come."

He raised a window as I appeared. It wasn't
broken and it lifted high enough for a guy to crawl
in without hurting himself – a skinny guy, that is.
Bonar wiggled through OK. Then I tried it. Well,
like I told you at the beginning, I've never been
thin. Not fat either, but just too wide to go through
that window without a struggle. I sucked myself in
to as tight a package as possible and squeezed
through. The monkey was sitting on a rafter over
our heads. Suddenly he chattered again, and was

off swinging out through a higher window.

We watched the monkey disappear and then tried to get a look around. Some of the windows were boarded up. The others were dirty and over-grown with vines or covered with spider webs so the place wasn't very bright. The fact that it was by now very cloudy outside didn't help any. In fact if you were in a corner away from the window you could barely see at all. A long hallway ran down the back of the building beside the locked door.

"Let's go and see what's down here," Bonar said. "Probably was once rooms for the soldiers," he added, sticking his head in the first of the rooms that opened off the hall.

"Yeah, it looks like a dormitory. It'd probably hold 20 men." There were several such rooms.

"This one still has the beds," Bonar called. "Two beds – upstairs and downstairs. What do you call them?"

"Bunks." The room was lined with five on each wall, some with the mattresses still on them. Where there were no mattresses I could see the ropes that took the place of springs. Not very comfortable, probably, but then this was the army. A lot of the ropes were hanging loose. Most of the windows were boarded over too, leaving a space above the boards of about two inches, through which there was enough light to see the beds.

"Smells musty." I began to feel kind of weird. There was a scraping noise outside. Probably just the wind blowing a branch against the metal roof. Anyway I said to Bonar, "Let's get out of here.

There's nothing to see anyway. Just old army relics. We'd better go." I wasn't scared. Just kind of edgy.

Bonar went on ahead of me and stopped.

"What's this?" He was kneeling down looking at the floor in a small closet. I bent over to have a look. The floor of the building was concrete but the closet floor was wooden. It was hinged on one side and bolted at the other. In fact it looked like the whole closet floor would lift up. A sturdy handle was built at one end.

"Wow! A trap door!"

"Help me, it's heavy." Bonar was pulling on the handle. We pulled as hard as we could and felt it begin to move.

"Looks like this whole closet is just built to hide this trap door. When the closet's closed you'd never know there was anything like this. Pretty smart!"

"Yeah, but why? I wonder where it goes or what it's for? C'mon, let's try again."

It took a bit of work but eventually we got the door up on its hinges. Stairs led down steeply into the semi-darkness below. We made our way down them cautiously. Cool air met us immediately.

"Hey, this is a basement, only narrow."

"It's a tunnel. Let's see what it goes to." The opening in the floor above us let in the only light. We could see the tunnel a few feet ahead and then nothing. We groped our way along the wall a step at a time. We'd gone about six or eight feet maybe when we hit a wall.

"That's it. The end of the tunnel," Bonar said.

"That's funny. Why build a tunnel that doesn't go anywhere?" My hand touched something on the wall. "Hey, what's this. Bonar, it feels like a lantern or fla.. Wait..." I hit the button my finger was touching and bingo! Light! All of a sudden we saw that the "wall" in front of us was really a door. Bonar turned the handle and the door opened slowly. "This tunnel does go somewhere!" I shivered at the thought.

"There's a whole room and... Wow!"

We both stared.

What we saw was a large appliance which I knew to be some kind of copier, and a table piled high with stuff. I walked one step closer and took a careful look. There was a camera set up, an offset printer over in the corner, a desk lamp, and a piece of glass on a sort of stand with a florescent strip light under it, and other things I couldn't identify. We couldn't speak for a minute.

Finally I saw Bonar lick his lips and in a small voice he said, "Phoney papers. It's for making phoney papers – visas and passports."

It made sense then. I remembered a book I had once read about a detective catching a forgery expert. This was all equipment for duplicating passports, making photos, pasting up phoney page layouts, the whole thing. The glass with the light under it I knew was for tracing signatures. They put the genuine writing on the glass with the bright light shining through and lay the paper they're trying to make on top of that and trace the signature. It was all here. I couldn't believe my eyes. I stepped closer and looked at some of the junk on the desk. Yes, there was an ink eradicator for removing writing.

"Wh..who...why would all this be here?" Bonar was about to touch the copy machine when I stopped him. "Don't touch anything. It'll get your finger-prints on it. That'll only confuse things if the police ever want to trace the culprit."

"Maybe all this is old stuff just stored here from the days the army used this building. Leftovers." I think he said it to make me feel better, because he didn't sound convinced.

"No, Bonar, I don't think so. Look at that camera. New. And that lamp. New. And what about the lock on the door, remember?" I stopped to think. "Be-sides, what about the lantern?"

"Oh, yes," Bonar agreed. "It has a good battery so someone must have used it recently and left it here."

"Oh, oh!" It suddenly hit me. "They left it be-cause they're ...coming...back. Bonar, let's get out of here."

CHAPTER

NINE

We closed the door to the room and hung the lantern up where it had been. Inch by inch we felt our way back along the wall toward the stairs. The darkness was eerie; I could almost feel it. Then I thought of something.

"Bonar, when we were this close to the stairs there was a bit of light from the entryway. How come now it's totally dark?"

"What do you mean?"

"If the door is open up above us there ought to be a bit of light here – dim, but not this dark. Remember?" It could mean only one thing. The trap door was closed.

I don't know if he was as scared as I suddenly was, but I admit I began to think the worst.

Together we groped our way up the steps one at a time, cautious but eager to reach that door.

"Must have blown shut with the wind. We'll just push it up."

"Alan," Bonar said after a minute, "it doesn't push open. I'm pushing with all my strength and it won't open." There was a tone of desperation in his hoarse whisper.

Don't panic, I told myself. *Darkness won't hurt you. Just stay calm.* To Bonar I said, "OK. Let's try together." I crawled up beside him on the second step. Somehow there was a little comfort in just being beside somebody.

"OK. Push. Again." We counted to three and gave it a heave.

"It's no use. Something's holding it at this end. The bolt must have slipped into place."

I was scared now. I mean really petrified because I knew the bolt couldn't just fall into place by accident.

"Somebody's locked it; we're trapped in here!" I don't know why I felt I had to whisper. A new wave of terror came over me and I tried not to give in to the fear.

We could yell for help and be dragged out by whoever locked us in here, and face goodness-knows-what, or say nothing and hope they'd go away – and remain trapped. Either way, the future wasn't very promising.

Then we heard a scratching sound on the floor above. A small sound I couldn't identify.

Bonar recognized it. "That monkey. The monkey's up there. He locked us in."

He shouted a few words in Indonesian. Silence. Had he run off and left us? Then a soft sound. He must be still nearby. Bonar said some more, loudly

enough for the monkey to know he meant business.
Then came the sound of the bolt wiggling in the
lock. *He's playing with it at least,* I thought. *Come
on, monkey, open it and leave it open.*

The bolt scraped and slid back and the soft
padded feet hurried away. We pushed cautiously.

"It's open! Let's go!" I was right behind Bonar as
we scrambled out. Even the dim light of dusk
through half-boarded windows seemed brilliant
compared to the basement. "Boy, am I glad you
were with me," I told Bonar. "I wouldn't have
known what to say to that monkey. I didn't even
know it was a monkey at first." The fear on his face
melted away into a big smile. We slapped each
other on the back in relief and congratulated ourselves on being free. All of a sudden I felt like we'd
been friends a long time.

"Come on, let's get out of here. We're not safe
yet." I headed back the way we came. I knew we'd
have to squeeze back through that window again;
but it'd be easier this time because I was a whole lot
more motivated to get out than I was to get in. I'd
make the squeeze all right if it killed me.

Suddenly we both stopped and blinked. The door
which had been locked on the outside with the new
lock was now flung wide open. In the doorway stood
a bow-legged man in shorts, a pointed straw hat on
his head. He had a new gold watch on his arm. I
looked beyond him out the door. Somehow I knew
what I'd see. There it was – blue roof and blue and
white checked flags, the licence plate in honor of
Mama still hanging limply by one wire. This was

the *becak* driver who'd been entering and reentering our lives for the past few days.

He was shouting something to Bonar who was backing away.

"He say, no. No escape. He kill us." I could tell by the way his English had suddenly deteriorated that Bonar was terrified.

The man began waving his hands and speaking Indonesian. I strained to pick out a few words but my mind was whirling and it all sounded fuzzy. He was motioning us back into the building.

Suddenly he switched to English for my benefit. "You go inside." He was standing between Bonar and the doorway, blocking his escape. He put one hand in his shirt and pulled out a revolver. Waving it at us both he was now clearly in control. There was no choice. "Walk".

My heart was pounding so hard I could hardly breathe. I could feel the blunt pressure of the gun in my back as he prodded us back into the dormitory section and pushed us into one of the large rooms. Motioning us to sit down on the floor and saying a few words to Bonar, he pulled a rope out of one of the old bed springs. It was pitch dark except for the crack above the window boards. The man was talking to Bonar as he lashed one rope around his ankles and brought the other end to his wrists, wrapping it around them and securing them behind his back. Bonar wasn't answering his tirade. He winced as the man tightened the wrist rope, but said nothing.

Now it was my turn. With all his effort at rope

tying and bending over, the man's coolie hat had
fallen off. As he approached me I saw his right ear.
A sick feeling washed over me. I'd seen that ear
before. This was the accomplice I had seen getting
in the car at Borobodur, the one who was somehow
linked to the passport forger in the airport. We
were in deep trouble.

With wide rope that seemed too strong to bend,
the man wrapped my feet and proceeded to tie my
hands. He knew what he was doing. Leaving both
of us in a heap in the corner, he said something to
Bonar and left.

For the first time since we'd been caught, we
dared to look at each other. Fear was as clear on
Bonar's face as it felt in my stomach.

"What's going on?" I whispered.

"He says we know too much. He will keep us
quiet."

I wiggled my back trying to get more comfortable. "What's he going to do with us now, did he
say?"

"No."

My mind was racing to put things together. A lot
of details were beginning to form some kind of
pattern. The *becak* driver could just be a local front-
man for the big operator. Probably the fat man was
a little higher up. Maybe, one of the buyers in
Jakarta. After all Bonar mentioned that he'd worked
for him once when he lived in Jakarta. Could both
of those be working for the really big man, the one
we saw at the airport?

Something about that guy seemed to scream at

me. Who was he? Should I be able to pick up some clue about him that I was overlooking? He had a lot of money, that was obvious. Quite successful at his work. He also had a briefcase with gold initials on it. TRA.

TRA... I let them run across my mind's eye a couple times till something jumped out at me. The picture of Bonar's uncle on his wall. It had been signed T R Arifin. Only coincidence. Bonar's uncle wouldn't be into anything shady. Or would he? Why not? I knew he wasn't a Christian, Bonar had said so. And I gathered there was something about him that Bonar hadn't liked. That's why he left home for Jakarta. And he did mention something about his uncle being in some kind of trouble once. Could that be it? It was a long shot and I knew I was grasping for anything to make sense.

We stopped talking. The ropes began to chafe our ankles.

I tried wiggling my wrists, contracting my muscles and bending my hand into a narrow shape to see if it eased the pain of the rope around my wrist. It made no difference. I wiggled my way backwards so my back rested against the wall. The concrete was cold against my back. A strong wind was blowing trees against the building and the sky was black. I shivered. I guess it was the combination of cold and fear. I knew I had to keep calm. I had to think. There must be some way to get out of this mess. Think. Think. Come on brain, get an idea.

I deliberately forced myself to be rational. My

parents would miss us eventually but they wouldn't be able to find us. They'd never know to look here. And Uncle Phil and Aunt Lori and Steve weren't at home. There was no way out that I could see.

CHAPTER

TEN

Neither of us spoke for the longest time. Gradually my heart slowed and I stopped shaking. My wrists were beginning to really hurt. More than that, I was beginning to put things together and come up with some disturbing conclusions. The picture on Bonar's wall kept coming back to my mind. And the picture of the "wanted" man on the immigration poster. The more I thought about it, the more I was sure they were of the same man, the man we had seen at the airport when we arrived. I didn't know how to bring up the subject.

"Bonar, are you all right?"

"Yes, all right."

"Bonar, I've seen this guy before," I began. I was almost afraid of what my own words would turn up. Like if we put all the facts on the table we wouldn't like what we figured out.

"Yeah, I know – that is the same *becak* driver that was following us the other day. The same one

we saw coming down here that night. But..."

"Yeah, but listen. I forgot to tell you this when it happened but I saw this guy at Borobodur. He didn't have his *becak* there of course, but he was getting into a car. I recognize him by his ear. Did you notice his funny ear?"

"Yes. Something wrong with it," Bonar nodded.

"Well, this guy was getting in a car with two men who'd been talking to each other earlier. I was only a few yards away and I heard them talking. One of them was the fat man who followed us in the *becak*. The other one... " I hated to say what I knew I had to say next. "Well, the other man I'd seen at the airport the day we arrived. He was in some kind of trouble. Later I saw his face on a leaflet in Se-marang. Something to do with immigration. I got thinking and... Bonar, I hate to tell you this, but I think it was your uncle." There, I'd told him. That was the hardest part.

Bonar looked shocked for a second, then angry.

"Bonar, you gotta believe me. I saw that picture of him in your room, remember? I didn't think anything of it then of course, but now I'm sure it was the same person."

"What did he look like, this man that you saw?"

"I can't describe him exactly, I just saw him briefly at the airport. Taller than usual. Well dressed. But mostly I noticed he had a heavy lock of hair that hung down on his forehead and mirror sunglasses, you know, the kind you can't see through to know if the person's looking at you or not. "

"I know; go on."

"Well, that's about all I noticed – oh, he had a mole on his cheek. And a beautiful briefcase of some kind of skin, with TRA in gold initials on the top. That's all I can remember. I wouldn't have recognized him in the immigration leaflet immediately – his hair was a bit different – until I drew sunglasses on him."

Bonar was nodding his head slowly as if he knew what I was going to say. "Yes, that sounds like my uncle. But my uncle is not here. He lives in Sumatra. Not on this island at all. It is impossible."

I could see why he was mad. But I was sure I wasn't mistaken. "No, it's not impossible for him to be here. You said yourself he travels a lot. And all the details make sense. Same initials. Traveler. Lots of money. And influence. And you said something about him being in trouble once before." I could see the truth was sinking in. "I don't want you to be mad, but I really think he's involved."

Bonar's anger was gradually being replaced with confusion. "Why? Why would he be talking to my ex-boss and this bad *becak* driver?"

"Well, my guess is your uncle Arifin and that fat man and this ...this phoney *becak* driver are together in whatever it is." A roll of thunder sounded in the distance.

"With that equipment we saw, I'd say the three of them are operating a phony passport racket," I went on. "Making false passports, and probably other papers too, for ... well, I don't know who for, but people that shouldn't have them or couldn't get them legally."

We were silent a few minutes. The thunder was closer now and a bolt of lightning followed.

Bonar shifted his tied arms as much as possible and leaned forward to talk in a serious whisper. "Alan, I didn't want you to know this about me, but I tell you now. We are friends."

"Sure, Bonar. What is it?"

"Your father's passport stolen in Jakarta ... I used to do that, steal passports. It was my job and, like I told you, the man who followed us in *becak* was my boss. There were five or six of us who worked for him. We just called him *bapak*. He paid us a little for each passport, then he would change it and sell it to somebody else for a big price – thousands of dollars. There is much money for a stolen passport. For him, not for me."

I couldn't think of what to say next. After a minute Bonar continued, "You're right about this stuff we saw. It is for making the phoney papers, and it is *bapak's* operation, I'm sure. But I didn't know my uncle was in on anything like that. I knew he was arrested once for something, but I didn't know what it was."

"Well, we've just stumbled across their headquarters." *Great*! I thought to myself. *Just great*! All because of chasing that stupid monkey. Now what? No wonder they're keeping us tied up; they want time to clear out of here before we go to the police and tell what we've seen.

"If they have time, they can move their 'office' and then, there'll be no evidence. And without evidence, who'll believe us. We're just two boys."

There was a sudden deafening crack of thunder, and lightning flashed across the room. Just for an instant everything was dazzlingly bright.

"But, Alan, if we go to the police and *bapak* gets caught, he will be sure I told them. He knows I'm here now, since he followed us the other day, so, since I escape from him, he will think... You know what I am trying to say?"

"Sure. He used you to do his dirty work for a while, you escaped from him and now you turn him in for revenge. In turn he either takes you back and forces you to stay with him to keep you quiet – after all, you were guilty yourself so he can hold that over you – or he... he shuts you up... some... other... way." My voice faded out. Was it possible he would actually kill Bonar? Or both of us?

"Alan, I don't know what he'd do if he gets mad enough. Besides, if you're right, my uncle is also involved in this."

Another crack of thunder silenced him for a moment. As soon as it was quiet Bonar spoke again, like there was something he really wanted to say, no matter what happened.

"I don't want you to think I had something to do with this. Since I came to McDonalds' to work, I became a Christian. Now I don't want anything to do with all that – or with *bapak*. Or even with my uncle if he's a criminal. But I can't turn him in to the police... He is my family.. . I'm scared, Alan, really scared."

"I know, Bonar, I believe you. And I'm scared too. I don't know what to do next." Then I thought of something I should have thought of long ago. "We'd better pray. Only God knows how to get us out of this mess."

Bonar nodded and I said, "Dear God, I'm sorry we didn't think of you before. I know you're with us. Please help us know what to do and, if it's your will, please get us out of here alive."

I felt a little bit better after that. We weren't in it alone any more. But we weren't free either. I tried to collect my thoughts.

"I guess the first thing is to get out of these ropes."

I wiggled my wrists furiously. Little by little; contract, relax. Contract, relax. Move thumbs. Wiggle, wiggle. Over and over. I was glad for the muscle control I'd developed in my arms from baseball. Keep on. There, could that be a little movement? The ropes didn't feel quite as tight as before. Yes, I could move my right wrist slightly. But only slightly. It would take forever at this rate. Still... I called over to Bonar to encourage him. "Keep working those ropes. We've got to get our hands free first thing we do."

"I cannot. It's hopeless."

"Mine isn't. I'm getting somewhere, I think." More wiggling. More flexing. There, I could move one wrist enough to bend my fingers up to touch the rope. Picking at it, I was able to find the end and push it back through the knot. It loosened! Working quickly now – I was feeling almost hopeful again – I slid it loose and pulled one hand free. The second hand was easy after that. I rubbed my wrists to take away the rope burns and restore circulation.

"Sit tight just a minute, Bonar. Let me get my feet undone here and then I'll help you." I tackled the heavy rope twined around my ankles. "This'll take a while. It's too tight."

Just as I said that, familiar footsteps sounded outside the door. I froze. In that instant I slipped my hands behind my back as if they were still tied and leaned back against the wall, hoping the man wouldn't make me move away and reveal my untied hands.

"Oh, God, please help him not to look," I prayed silently.

Our *becak* "friend" stepped through the doorway and looked at us. He began talking to Bonar, sounding agitated. As he spoke the man flashed a light around, letting the beams play on us. He seemed satisfied that we were still suffering sufficiently. Flicking off the light, he strode toward the door and left. We heard the key turn in the lock again.

Whew! That was close. "Thank you again, Lord," I said, out loud this time. I looked around, trying to get a good look at our prison. Maybe something would give me an idea.

"I've read a lot of stories and seen a lot of TV shows where people get themselves out of a bad situation like this, and it always looks so easy," I told Bonar. "But when it comes right down to *me,* I can't see any way out. Surely if we put our heads together we can think of something."

I was very glad for Bonar's company about that time. It helped to have somebody with you. But I wished there was more light in the place. The crack above the window boards let in only a shaft and the sky was overcast. In fact, except for the lightning it was almost dark.

With my eyes I followed the dim light into every corner, over the cement floor, five sets of bunks, one... suddenly another flash of lightning blazed, longer this time.

"What's that?" I said, as much to myself as to Bonar. I scooted along on my seat towards an object I'd spotted on the floor. Under one bed, just in the shadow behind the leg, was a familiar shape.

CHAPTER

ELEVEN

"I need another bolt of lightning," I said. Almost on cue thunder came and a brilliant flash lit up the room and glanced off something shiny and metallic. I spread myself out flat, my feet still tied together, and scooted myself along on my stomach until I could reach under the bed. My fingers folded around something I recognized.

"Hey, guess what. It's my knife! My Swiss Army knife that monkey stole. He came here with it and hid it!" I was almost shouting now over the roar of thunder and rain. "Boy, am I glad to get this back. We might have a chance yet if I can get these ropes off."

"Hurry up," Bonar reminded me. "I'm still tied up."

"Yeah, I'm coming, I'm coming. As soon as I can get my feet free and get you untied we can get out of here."

Working furiously on the ankle ropes I was able

to saw through enough to slip out one leg, then the other. Free! There. At least that was done. Now to help Bonar... I freed his hands and feet.

"OK," I said, trying to sound calm. "We're locked in a boarded up dormitory with only my knife. What can we do to escape?"

"What can that knife of yours do?" Bonar asked. "I remember you were showing us some of it before the monkey stole it."

I shrugged. I didn't see how it'd be much help to us right then but I didn't have any better idea and besides, I was pretty proud of that knife, so I obliged. "Well, it has three sizes of blades, a pair of scissors, a small saw — like I said, it will actually cut down a tree."

"Never mind, never mind. Think of what it can do for us," Bonar interrupted.

"And it has a bottle opener, a corkscrew, a fork and here's an ivory toothpick that slides in the end like this." I demonstrated. "Everything you need for being lost in the woods but not much for being locked in an old army camp." I had to admit it didn't exactly look hopeful.

"If it's big enough..." Bonar was thinking out loud. "Your saw. Is it big enough to cut through those boards?" He was pointing to the slabs of wood covering the windows.

I was doubtful. Those were pretty thick and there was no way to get a start on them. Not like cutting off the ropes or attacking a sapling. I considered other alternatives.

"Maybe we could cut a hole right here below this

door handle and reach our fingers out and undo the lock." As soon as I'd said it I realized that wasn't a good idea.

"Even if you could make a hole big enough to put your fingers through, we couldn't reach the lock," Bonar said.

I thought again. The walls and floor were solid concrete. No hope there. No trap doors to lift out. Not that I wanted to see another one for a while anyway! There was nothing except those boarded-up windows.

Bonar had climbed up onto an upper bunk by now and was feeling around the window area. I climbed up beside him. Sawing through those boards still looked like our only chance.

There was a lull in the storm now. The racket outside seemed to be less. I stopped sawing and surveyed my progress.

"We're getting there. If we can cut one end loose we can kick it back and make a hole big enough to crawl through."

"I'll saw some," Bonar offered.

"Wait. Wait a minute. Do you hear that?" I felt a new wave of panic sweeping over me. "A car. Listen!"

Bonar nodded, motioning for silence. A vehicle was driving into the camp yard. Probably a truck, I decided. It swung around the end of the wing where our dorm was and up the other side to the door.

We were both stiff with fright as well as the effort of trying to listen and not be heard. We held

ourselves motionless, frozen. Men's voices jabbered
in Indonesian. Lights shone. Something scraped.
Then men entered the building, walked a few feet
and stopped. There were loud voices now and
footsteps getting further away, like going downstairs.

I let out a long breath and felt my muscles loosen
slightly. I knew what was happening. Those guys
were going down to their basement hideaway to get
the printing and photography equipment. Bonar
realized it too. We listened to the struggle of haul-
ing a box up the stairs, through the trap door and
out of the building. Then a clatter and bang and the
box was on the truck. Same process repeated.

There was no doubt in my mind. They were
loading up their stuff and moving out. I thought
they had picked a good night to do it – no one would
see or hear them in this storm. Our best chance of
escape was to wait till they left and then break out.
On the other hand, if we were going to catch them
we'd have to get out of here and get the police before
they pulled out and disappeared.

That gave me an idea. If it's good for them, it was
good for us for the same reason.

"Bonar," I whispered excitedly. "Come on, let's
get out of here while we can. The storm will be our
cover; it'll hide our noise."

He nodded and set to work with new effort on the
window boards. The little blade got hot but we took
turns and kept on sawing as quickly as possible.
Back and forth, back and forth. The hum of the tiny
saw was swallowed up by the roar of rain on the

roof.

"There. That's it," The board came loose from the nails at the end. "Now we kick it back. Let's both kick together – hard. Ready? One...two...*three.*"

We swung our legs with all our might. The board swung back on its one fastened end, splintered and broke. We now had a space about 15 inches deep and two feet wide across the top of the window.

Bonar stretched up and stuck his head over the top.

"We're ten feet off the ground!" he reported in whispered desperation. "How are we going to get down?"

"Jump. It's our only chance."

When the roar of the storm lessened periodically I could hear the men out the other side of the building so I knew they were still there. Fortunately they couldn't see our window cutting operation.

"Bonar, if they pull out of here before we get a message to somebody we'll never catch them. They'll be long gone and we won't know which direction."

"OK," Bonar said. "I'll go first. There's some bushes, even small trees; maybe we can sort of climb down. Run straight for our bikes and out to the main road."

"Oh, Bonar. We'd better pray."

He nodded. We closed our eyes and I made it short – something like, "Oh God, you know where we are. Please help us get out of here and get help. Amen. Now go," I urged in the same breath. "I'm right behind you."

Bonar hung on to the top of the opening and swung one leg over. Then the other. He slipped over the side and was gone. I heard a crackle of bushes. Then rain pelted against the building again, covering all other sound.

I followed. I wasn't aware of being terrified – just desperate. No choice. Got to go. *Out,* I told myself. As I slipped my second leg over I grabbed for the branch of the tree beside me. At least it could break my fall even if it wasn't strong enough to support me. Rain pelted with a deafening roar on the roof. I was already soaked but I was thankful for the noise it provided. I heard Bonar's feet on the gravel and I hoped he had gotten away, but I couldn't hear any other clues. Nothing but more rain and rumbling thunder. I felt the tree sway wildly under my weight. My hands were wet, the trunk slippery. I landed on the ground with a jolt.

All of a sudden a sharp pain stabbed my ankle. I had fallen in the bushes. The branches and weeds growing thickly around the bottom of the wall were prickly and sharp. If I could stand up at least my head and shoulders might be above them and I could keep my eyes from getting scratched. But as I tried to stand my ankle gave a sharp warning of pain. "Ouch!" I must have said it out loud because suddenly a voice called out. I didn't need to understand the words to know it was directed at me.

I clapped my hand over my mouth and grabbed my ankle to steady it. They must have stationed one of their cronies on this side of the building as a lookout. Fear took away the pain in my ankle. I stayed low, cowering behind the weeds on the wet ground. My ankle kept sending shooting pains up my leg. Prickles poked me all over. I was muddy and soaked to the skin. I wanted to change to a more comfortable position but I was too scared to move. The voice called again, then muttered something and I heard footsteps leaving. Then the rain took over again, pounding harder, blocking out every other sound. The man must have given up and gone back to helping his friends load the stuff onto the truck. I didn't dare check to see. I tried to keep from hurting my ankle any more than it was. I took advantage of the noise of the storm to move slightly, so I was lying flat with my ankle straight.

It was only now that I began to think about the predicament I was in. Bonar was gone. Here I was all alone, with a bunged-up ankle, not able to say anything to defend myself if I was caught... Even without hurting my ankle I wouldn't have been able to get away with those guys watching like they were, especially now that one of them was suspicious. Then it dawned on me what a good thing it was that I hadn't gone after all. Now I was right on the spot to see what they did and where they went. Otherwise we'd have no track of them.

I began to pull myself along, slowly, waiting for gusts of rain and thunder to cover my sound. I reached the corner where the dormitory wing extended. If I could see beyond that I'd have a better view. I pulled myself along cautiously another three feet or so. I still couldn't see what they were doing but I could see the truck's headlights and hear the operation clearly. I could tell they were hoisting the crates onto the truck. Then there was a bang, a metallic, jarring sound and voices talking. *That's it,* I thought. *They've closed the tailgate. They're going to leave.* I'd have given anything right then for an instant understanding of Indonesian. Then I heard some words I did know.

"...*ke Semarang.*" Then a few more sentences and then "*Semarang, jam dua.*" The rest was lost in a new surge of wind. But that voice sounded familiar – or was it? Maybe it was all in my mind. I lay motionless. I told myself to concentrate on remembering the words and not think about how miserable I was. I said them over, trying to force my mind to think. "*Semarang. Jam dua. Semarang. Jam dua.*"

I remembered the counting lesson Bonar had given me in the car, "..*satu, dua, tiga...*" *Dua* was two. Something about two. The men must be climbing into the truck from the sounds of it. I dared a peek. One man was climbing in the driver's door with a flashlight. I saw him reach up and push his glasses up on his nose and shove a lock of hair back. I knew that gesture was familiar but I couldn't take time to think where I'd seen it. I must concentrate on what was happening.

The motor started, coughed, spluttered into a steady growl and they pulled out. The headlight beams moved, turned, and shone straight for me. I hoped the bushes and weeds were thick enough to hide me in spite of being blown by the wind. The truck passed just a few feet away from me. All I could get a look at were the tires. Mud flew up around them as they rolled past. I saw no writing, no name, nothing to identify it. I certainly couldn't see the driver. But as they went on by I raised my head just enough to peek through the grass and see the licence plate on the back. AV 4 5987.

I moved a little so I could watch them go down the army camp road and out to the highway. There he would have to turn, I knew. I could barely see the lights in the distance, but – yes, he turned to the right. He's going back toward town. All right. It wasn't much, but it was all I could find out. Maybe it would help some. I knew now where I had seen that glasses-pushing gesture before.

The truck faded into the darkness. I had nothing now to keep my mind off my ankle and the muddy, prickly nest I was lying in. And the shock of the realization that it was David from Uncle Phil's university driving that truck.

CHAPTER

TWELVE

"Come on, come on, please. Hurry up." Bonar must have gotten some help by now. Where were they? I figured surely as soon as my folks knew where I was, they'd come. My ankle was getting stiff. It must be swelling, I thought, but I couldn't see to examine it. "Hurry up, Bonar, Dad, Uncle Phil – somebody. Hurry."

Then I remembered. There was somebody with me. God was there. I'd forgotten Him in all the events of the last few minutes. "God," I said out loud, "Thanks for reminding me that you're still here. Thanks for keeping me from being injured any worse than I am. Or being shot by those crazy guys," I added. "Now please help me get home."

Maybe I could make it to my bike, if I hopped. I hobbled to my feet to try it, but at that moment more lights came down the road into the camp. I ducked back into the grass. Had the guys come back for something? More equipment? Me? I made a little peephole through the weeds so I could see without being seen.

Then I recognized Uncle Phil's car! I pulled myself out of the bushes and propped myself up on one foot. Hobbling toward the gateway I waved, and the car stopped.

Out jumped my dad and Uncle Phil!

"Boy, I'm glad to see you!" I said. "I guess Bonar told you what happened?"

"He told us enough for us to come and get you," Dad answered. "Here let's get out of the rain." He helped me into the car, loaded my bike in the back and we were off.

"Now fill us in on the details," Uncle Phil said as we headed back to the house.

I told him what I knew and what we had figured out. "But there's something real funny going on. I saw David there. He's driving the truck, I'm sure. I know it sounds crazy."

Uncle Phil said nothing as he headed the car towards town in the storm. I didn't know whether he believed me or not but I was sure I was not mistaken. "I can give the police the truck licence number," I offered.

"Might be helpful," Uncle Phil said. "Maybe we'd better go to the police station before we go home so you can tell them all you know. Think you're up to it?"

"Sure. I can hop. I don't think my ankle's broken – just twisted probably."

When we walked into the police post Bonar and Yakob were giving details very carefully as a policeman typed a report.

"They've put out a search warrant on the men, but we don't really know where to look," Yakob explained in English.

"Let me tell you what I found out," I said, a little pleased with myself in spite of my sore ankle. "The truck licence number is AV 4 5987." The policeman scribbled quickly as I talked. "And something else. They're going to Semarang. I heard them say, 'ke Semarang'. And then I understood, 'jam dua'. That's all I could pick up."

"Thank you very much." One policeman quickly radioed the information to the squad car. The other one listened as I repeated my side of the story. Everything I could think of. Bonar translated as I told it.

When we felt there was nothing more we could do we headed for home. I was beginning to realize how tired I was.

Mom was waiting for us when we arrived. She fussed over my ankle of course, and told me I should be ashamed of myself getting into something like that in the first place and how lucky I was I didn't break every bone in my body and so on, like mothers do. But I was so relieved to be sitting there alive and in one piece I didn't mind, and eventually she did get my ankle feeling better. After a bath and change of clothes I felt a whole lot different.

Much as I wanted to stay awake and hear the outcome of the whole thing I couldn't fight the drowsiness that enveloped me. Before I knew it I was asleep. I had to wait till the next day to hear how things turned out.

"You were right, Alan," Dad told me at breakfast. "You two had it figured out. Bonar's uncle Arifin was the big boss, over the whole operation. The *becak* driver was really an accomplice who was stationed locally. Driving a *becak* was just a cover. Gave him a good way to move around in the town without suspicion and keep an eye on things. They chose to do the work here because it was less conspicuous, smaller town, up country, that sort of thing. Takes the pressure off the guy in Jakarta a bit."

"That was the fat man, right?"

"Right. He's the one that acted as middleman. They operate a big immigration scam – forged passports, visas, whatever." Uncle Phil continued, "They were hoping to get the equipment into a new hiding place in Semarang at two am. Fortunately the police got them before then. That is, they got two of them – Fat Man and his *becak*-pedaling accomplice. But the guy at the top, Arifin, wasn't with them. He's too slippery to let himself get caught."

Footsteps sounded in the backyard and in a moment Yakob's big smiling face appeared around the door.

"Thanks for all your help last night, Yakob," Uncle Phil said to him. "For taking Bonar to the police and so on. I guess you heard all the details before we did."

"Yes, but I also have some more since then, bad news, I'm afraid. I hate to tell you this, Mr McDonald but... well, it seems David ...is in on this too. He helped make arrangements for the Semarang connection and sort of paved the way with immigration. None of us suspected. His work with immigration for the faculty and missionaries gave him the perfect opportunity ...I'm sorry to have to tell you that."

Uncle Phil frowned and shook his head. "So it's true then. You were right, Alan. I was hoping you were mistaken..." It seemed he suddenly looked older. "I'm sorry to hear that, Yakob. Did you get a chance to talk to him?"

"Only a few words. He needed the money, he says. He didn't want to say much."

Uncle Phil looked at Dad. "Needed the money. Yes, I'm sure he did. Too bad he was willing to go to such ends to get it."

He shook his head slowly and rubbed a handkerchief over his forehead before he added, "And he claimed to be a Christian. I guess he was just blending in... "

Dad nodded sympathetically.

"Oh, here," Yakob said suddenly. "I've got something for Mr Carter. You'll be glad to see this." He handed Dad his passport.

"Thank you!" Dad exclaimed. "Where did you get this? Is it still all right?"

"Perfectly all right. The police got it back before the thieves had had a chance to mess it up or tear out the picture."

Dad was so relieved he kept looking at it as if he'd never seen it before.

"After Bonar left Alan at the army camp," Yakob continued, "he came cycling here as fast as he could to get help for Alan of course, and then came on over to my place and told me what was going on and asked if I would go with him to the police. But you should have heard Bonar when we got there. He did more than just say tell them what you two had found; he gave the police *bapak's* working code name and told all he knew about the operation from his past experience. Even admitted his involvement with it. The police were so grateful for his help I think they're going to ignore his part in past operations."

"What about his uncle Arifin?" I asked. "He was the ringleader, wasn't he?"

"Yes, and he wasn't new to the police. They'd been watching his activities for quite a while. Now they have enough to put him away for a long time – if they can catch him."

"What if he gets his hands on Bonar in the meantime? As long as he's on the loose, Bonar could be in real danger."

"I told Bonar that. But he was more interested in you getting your passport back safely, and he knew they would have to get it back quickly, before it was altered, if they were going to get it at all."

Dad didn't say much. He was quiet a minute and then he said softly, "Tell him I'm very grateful."

I guess we saw a lot of Java the rest of our vacation. I don't remember. After that, everything else seemed kind of tame.

The day before we left for home Bonar and I sat

outside in the backyard and talked a bit. We relived our escapade of course, and talked about school, world cup soccer – all sorts of things. We have a lot in common really. Seemed unbelievable that only a couple weeks before I was afraid to get to know him. I don't know why I thought he'd be all that different from me! Anyway, now I kind of hated to say goodbye to him.

Besides, we were both aware that his Uncle Arifin was still free, and very angry! If Bonar was nervous about that he didn't say much about it.

"Wish we could have seen more of this country. We only saw one island."

"Come back. Next time I'll show you around some of the other islands. Like Sumatra. It's beautiful... Lake Toba, mountains, white tigers. Or Bali. Long sandy beaches..."

"Whoa! Enough. I'm coming, I'm coming." I laughed. Meanwhile I knew I had to go back to the same old things. I could see Josh on the first day of school, sporting a new summer tan, with a circle of friends around him, laughing and carrying on. I knew it'd be just as hard as ever to resist his suggestions for what he called fun – even when I knew I should. And I could just hear the kids in the lunch room spouting off with all their obscene language and jokes – and me in the middle, deciding whether to say nothing or stick my neck out and risk being jumped on, verbally, by everybody else. Lots of chances to be "salt" whether I wanted to be or not. It was something I knew I had to work on.

"Hey, Bonar, maybe you and I could pray for

each other sometimes and write to each other once in a while."

He smiled and clapped me on the back. "Sure. That's what friends are for!"

"Well, if I did nothing else during this visit I can see I taught you more English!"

He laughed. "That and a few other things."

"Bonar, do you think you'll stay here and work for the McDonalds'?"

"Yes. For now at least. When I finish school maybe I'll go to university somewhere and then who knows...? But," he paused, "I will go back to Sumatra for a visit one day and talk to my uncle. I will tell him I am now a Christian."

"I'd just keep out of his way if I were you. After you told enough to crack his whole operation and get the police on his trail, he's not going to be happy to see you!"

"I know. But I have to tell him."

I shrugged. "Okay, I guess you're right, but I only hope he doesn't get his hands on you first."

He nodded and said nothing for a minute. Then he smiled and said, "I think if he gets arrested the Christians at the university will have more freedom. For them it would be good."

"Yeah, and for you too."

We had been home three weeks or so when we got my Aunt Lori's letter. It said the usual, "So glad you came" etc. and talked about the heavy rains they were having. Then Mum said, "Listen to this, everybody. Phil says they've managed to get charges dropped on David and have had a good opportunity to talk with him." She started reading again, "... said he needed the money, but he has confessed his connection and seems to be genuinely repentant. We believe he will really come to put his trust in Christ soon. Yakob is a real help to him these days, and we're praying for them both.

"And the day after you left, they arrested Arifin. Caught him in Jakarta. Sounds like he'll be behind bars for years. With Arifin in jail, his influence on the university is gone so the student Christian fellowship group has already begun to grow. They have asked one of our missionaries in town to speak at their next retreat. And, imagine this, there has even been a rumor that the university might want a foreign Christian to teach on the faculty there in the future. Just what we've hoped for!"

"And Bonar says to tell Alan he is saving his wages to buy a Swiss army knife – one with a saw blade."

"All right!" I laughed. "Smart boy!"

"So your snooping paid off," Deb said, tossing a cushion my way. I grabbed it and threw it back.

"I told you it would some day. Aren't you glad I was there?"

"I guess so." She shrugged. "I'm glad *I* was there, I'll tell you that. I had a good time. It's really hard to tell the kids at school about it though. They have such weird ideas about Indonesia and ask all sorts of dumb questions."

I thought I saw a twinkle in Mom's eye as she said, "Is that so?"